# THE SCENT OF REVENGE

*Book Two of The Patterns Series*

*Russell F. Moran*

Coddington Press
Copyright © 2015 by Russell F. Moran
Printed in the United States of America

ISBN: 0996346635
ISBN: 978-0-9963466-3-4

Edited by Brenda Judy
www.PublishersPlanet.com

Cover Design by Erin Kelly
http://erinkelly.webs.com/

www.MoranCom.com

This book is dedicated to those who suffer from Alzheimer's and other forms of dementia, and especially to their families who suffer along with them.

# ACKNOWLEDGEMENTS

Writing may be a lonely craft, but no work comes to daylight without the input from many people. As always, I thank my wife, Lynda, for her attentive reading and re-reading of my many drafts. I also thank my eagle-eyed friend, John White, for his proofreading and editing. And finally, I thank my editor, Brenda Judy. Brenda has an amazing ability to jump back and forth from the big picture to the tiniest detail. She is a pro.

# AUTHOR'S NOTE

You will find a **Cast of Characters** after the last chapter of the book. It can be frustrating to come across a character on page 250, who you first met on page 25, especially if you've put the book down for a few days. I've seen this done in Russian novels, and I happily add a cast of characters to *The Scent of Revenge*.

# CHAPTER ONE

"I almost lost you. I almost lost you for good. I can't stand this, Rick. I can't take it anymore. If you think you're marked for death, why do you have to help them?"

"What are you talking about?"

"What am I talking about? You just spent three days in the hospital hooked up to a cardiac monitor. You're 42 years old and in great physical shape, and you just had a friggin heart attack. *That*'s what I'm talking about."

A tear rolled down her face as Ellen looked at her coffee. She reached for the remote and turned off the TV.

The anchorman had just announced the latest terrorist attack on the United States, the first one in a week—a commuter train in Chicago was bombed and it derailed on a bridge. Terrorist attacks have been on a sickening rise since the infamous day of October 15, the worst day since 9/11. The attacks came so often we were becoming emotionally numb to the details. News stories of death and destruction were as familiar as weather reports.

It was Sunday, and we both had the day off.

With all of the insanity in my life, Ellen is the center of my universe. Just being with her calms me down. We've been married for three years, and I'm as much in love with her today as the day I proposed. I hate to see her upset. She's told me that when I'm in pain, she's in pain, and that's exactly the way I feel about her. I can't stand seeing her upset.

Love at first sight sounds hackneyed, but when I first met Ellen at a charity fundraiser, that's exactly what it was. She's 38 years old, has medium-length blond hair, and beautiful pale green eyes. Ellen's a fitness nut, and has the figure to show for it. Under her left eye is a slight scar from a fall she took as a kid. But now it looks like a dimple, especially when she smiles, which is often. I once told her that the prettiest thing about her face was the scar. I'm not the greatest with words. Good-looking women are all around, but Ellen is different, or at least I think so. She has a warmth about her that just kind of radiates. She cares about people. Once, as we walked down the street near our apartment, she saw a woman drop a bag of groceries on the other side of the street—*the other side of the street*—so naturally, ducking traffic, Ellen crossed the street to help the woman. I followed, of course, but Ellen led the way to help the complete stranger with her groceries.

Life plays out in strange ways, ways that we often can't control. Three years ago, I was about to leave my apartment to go to a book signing. My old friend, Mickey Giordano, had just launched his latest novel. The afternoon before the event, Mickey was riding his bike when a squirrel darted in front of him. He swerved to avoid it, jumped a curb, and fell against a hydrant, fracturing his leg. Mickey texted me from the hospital to say the signing was cancelled. Since I had already planned to go out for the evening, I figured I'd go to a charity fundraiser that I also had an invitation to, so I changed into a suit. The event was to raise money for children's cancer research, something I always supported. That's where I met Ellen. Had that squirrel not ran in front of Mickey's bike, Ellen and I would never have met. To this day, I keep a brass statuette of a squirrel on our mantel with a nameplate in front of it: "Yenta."

I remember that night like it was yesterday. While Ellen and I chatted, a guy bumped into my arm, spilling my wine on Ellen's dress. "I'm sorry," she said, "let's get you a refill." *She* was sorry, not for the wine on her dress, but for *my* inconvenience. That's Ellen.

I'm an FBI agent, and I specialize in counterterrorism. I have a lot of weird stress in my life. Since the attacks of 10/15, I've lived a life of anxiety. But there's one part of my life that centers me, that makes me happy: my wife, Ellen.

After serving with the Marines in Iraq, I wasn't sure what I wanted to do, so I used my GI Bill to go to law school after I mustered out with the rank of captain. While I was in law school, I met a recruiter with the FBI, and it's been my life since. I was worried that I wouldn't pass the physical, having taken a bullet in my left arm in a firefight. Even though I passed, I still get a nasty pain in my arm occasionally. The bullet hit me inside my upper left arm, missing my heart by four inches. It's crazy what you think about sometimes, but it's occurred to me that if I'd been killed, I never would have met Ellen. That's a thought worse than death.

Ellen got up and refilled our coffee cups. She sat down at the table, looked into my eyes, reached over, and squeezed my hand.

I got up, pulled my chair next to hers, and put my arm around her.

"Hey, it wasn't a heart attack. The doctor said it was just a rare occurrence of atrial fibrillation, just a fluttering. No big deal. The FBI has strict rules about health issues, and that's why I was in the hospital for three days. The doctor didn't even put me on medication. I'm fine, hon. I just wish to hell you'd stop worrying."

"Rick, ever since President Reynolds announced that World War III has begun, you've taken it on as if it's your own goddam private war, as if winning it is up to you. You're the best agent in the FBI, but you can't take this on alone. We live in a world where terror is no longer news, and it's taking a big toll on you. I'm not going to let your job kill you. Hey, dickhead, say something."

"I love you. That's all I have to say."

"I love you too, honey, but I want to hear what the hell you're going to do to stay calm. I know it's your job to fight this war, but you've got to take care of yourself, and it's going to start right now."

Ellen got up, walked across the room to the breakfront, and pulled out a yellow pad.

"Okay, handsome, I'm the architect and you're my client. Together, we're going to design the new Rick Bellamy."

"This is getting me nervous."

"Pay attention, Mr. Client. We're about to do some preliminary sketches. Number one, yoga. I can teach you right here so you don't have to go to class. It's the best form of exercise I've found, and I've tried everything. Number two is meditation—every day for at least 20 minutes. I can teach you that too. Number three is more sex."

"Why don't we make that number one?"

"Done," she said as she pinched my knee and made a note on her pad.

"Number four," she said, "you and I should continue with that novel we're writing. We can have a manuscript ready for the editor in three months if we do 500 words a day.

"Number five," Ellen continued, "the telephone."

"The telephone?"

"Yes, the goddam telephone. Every time your phone rings, your face looks like you just stepped in dog shit. I can tell that you're expecting bad news whenever you answer it. So, here's my question: who's your favorite comedian?"

"Jerry Seinfeld, why?"

"I'm going to make up a list of jokes I found on the Internet for you to carry on an index card. I sometimes use Jerry Seinfeld jokes when I give a talk. Every time your phone rings, read one of the jokes, and imagine that Jerry Seinfeld is about to tell it. Great choice, by the way. He's my favorite too. Now you'll laugh at the scary cell phone whenever it rings. I want you to do the same thing before you turn on the TV. As the anchorman is about to announce the latest bombing, at least you'll start by laughing."

"Laughing at the telephone and TV? I like that."

"Number six," she said, "is more aerobic exercise. Good for the mind, and it calms you too. We have the treadmill in the guest-room, and I want you to do at least a half-hour a day."

Ellen walked over to the photocopy machine in the corner of the den. She put her list on the flatbed, made a paper copy, and then scanned the document to save it as a file. Ellen amazes me. She has an incredibly organized mind, with a memory that never quits. I've seen her at work in architectural planning meetings. She can recite a lengthy list of items without referring to her notes.

She handed me the original.

"Here, hon, our plan for the new Rick Bellamy."

I guess a lot of people who have been married for only three years think their marriage is special. I know it is for me and Rick.

A lot of things about our respective jobs seem contradictory. I'm an architect and my work is relatively predictable from day to day. Sure, I have crises occasionally, but it's not an occupation that I'd consider dangerous. Well, yes, last year I was kidnapped and almost killed by some Islamist extremists, and the reason that happened was because of an architectural project I was working on. Long story. I think the work of an architect is rather peaceful. Fascinating and remunerative, but peaceful.

Rick, on the other hand, is a warrior. That's right, he's a warrior. As an FBI agent, his work mainly involves investigation, not gun play. But our world is in turmoil, and Rick's work as a counter-terrorism specialist puts him in harm's way—a lot.

On 10/15, the forces of radical Islam declared war on America and the West; not by a formal decree, but by action. On that day, seven commuter trains and five commercial buildings were bombed, along with the people in them. Within a couple of weeks, two luxury cruise ships were blown up and sunk. In the next few months, more trains were attacked, two college football games were bombed, and, in the biggest terror spectacular of all, a plane loaded with explosives crashed into the Super Bowl game just before kickoff. Rick and I were supposed to be at the Super Bowl, but we couldn't get there because of a blizzard in New York. Our seats were beneath the broadcast booth that blew up and fell. We both would have died.

The attacks of 10/15 changed the world.

Even in a world of terror, my job comes at me slowly. A prospective client calls and we have a meeting, and then another meeting. Once we sign a contract, my fun begins as I start work on the new project. It all flows in a predictable way.

There's nothing predictable about my husband's work. Most of us wake up in the morning, check our to-do list, and have a pretty good idea of what our day will look like. It's not that way with Rick's job. He may flick on the TV to see the morning news, and an anchorman announces something that Rick has to jump on immediately. That's why I insisted he look at a joke before he answers the phone or turns on the television.

Rick is a dedicated man, and that's one of the many things I admire about him. He doesn't believe in leaving some shit for the next guy to pick up. Rick is waging a personal war against people who want to kill us, and he wants to win the war. Ever since the terrorist attacks of 10/15 last year, Rick's job has spun into an almost unearthly series of crises, one after another. I know it's silly to think that the radical killers are trying to personally hurt Rick, but I want to stand between them and him.

When he was hospitalized for his heart flutters, that did it for me. No way in hell was I about to watch the man I love burn himself out for his job. I think he's serious about my action plan for calming his overactive emotions. I know he's serious about the number one item on my plan—making love. I sure am. It's not that we need a reminder, because it's something we do a lot, a whole lot, but it was just kind of fun to put it in writing.

I want Rick around for a long time. I love him, I admire him. He's also my friend, probably my best friend.

# CHAPTER TWO

Today is Friday, April 1, and I'm about to meet with New York FBI Director Barbara Auletta, my boss. Thanks to Ellen, my day started off great. We took care of number one last night, and I started the day with a half-hour on the treadmill, followed by some new yoga exercises that Ellen taught me. After that, I meditated for 20 minutes. Then we did some speed writing on our novel, hitting the 500-word mark in 45 minutes. My cell phone rang at 7:30, and I envisioned Jerry Seinfeld—"Two guys walk into a bar…"

I could do without Ellen about as easy as I could do without oxygen.

At 8:45 a.m., I sat in Barbara Auletta's office waiting for her and sipping a cup of decaf (another one of Ellen's ideas). Barbara's office was tastefully decorated with warm colors. The walls were beige and the carpet a light brown. Across from her desk were two leather arm chairs for visitors. At about 600 square feet, the office was large. A round conference table with six chairs occupied the corner.

Barbara walked in. She's a thin, pretty woman, 5'11", about 55 years old with short brown hair. She has a relaxed way about her, which I find amazing, considering her job. Barbara has a well-earned reputation as a by-the-books taskmaster, but I find her easy to work with. I think of her as a friend, not just a superior.

She's also tough as hell. A few years ago, Barbara and I were making an arrest. I was busy with one of the two men and Barbara went to cuff the other. After she tripped the guy, she slammed her knee into the small of his back and put on the cuffs like a sailor handling a line. And he was a big man. She stays in shape with a vigorous workout every day. Barbara came up through the ranks, and is now one of the senior officials in the bureau.

"I'm glad you're sitting, Rick. You've heard about the United Airlines plane crash at Newark Airport? Over 300 people killed."

"Of course," I said, "it's all over the TV."

"It wasn't just terrorism," Barbara said, "but something we've been worried about. The plane was taken down by a surface-to-air missile, a SAM."

Since 10/15, terrorist attacks in the United States have become as common as weather reports on the radio. Besides the constant bomb attacks, we narrowly avoided a massive bombing of five shopping malls across the country. Ellen designed the malls, and she helped us to stop the plan in its tracks. As the plot unfolded, Ellen was kidnapped by al-Qaeda. It was the worst time in my life. Thank God she was rescued by a SWAT team. Ellen pitched in by shooting two of her abductors. As I've said before, Ellen is gentle and kind, but she's also a tough customer.

Never a week goes by without a new terrorist event. President Reynolds took to the airwaves and announced that World War III had started. Yes, he actually announced that we were in World War III. At first, a lot of people thought that Reynolds was overreacting and being melodramatic. But as the incidents picked up in frequency and the body toll mounted, people realized that Reynolds was correct, that the world really was at war. But it's a war unlike anything we ever dreamed of. It's a war that wasn't declared by an enemy, because the enemy is a diffuse army of self-actors, not beholden to any nation state, although supported by plenty of them.

"Barbara, do we have any idea who was involved?" I thought this was a stupid question, but I had to ask it.

"No Rick. We know it was a SAM from a video that someone took as the plane came in for a landing. We know where the missile came from, a field of tall grasses about a half-mile from the airport. The missile shooter escaped before the police got there. Buster's on his way. We're about to find out what the CIA knows about surface-to-air missiles."

Barbara had no sooner finished her sentence when the desk intercom buzzed. "Agent Atkins is here to see you, Madam Director."

Buster walked in. Tall, at six feet, thin and impeccably dressed in a spring suit, Buster is an amazing spook, which is what spies like to call themselves. His real name is Gamal Akhbar, also known as Charles Atkins, also known as God-knows-what. Buster's the lead CIA agent for counterterrorism matters, and I often work with him. Thanks to some solid leadership at the top of both agencies, the line between the CIA and the FBI often blurs. Because he's fluent in Arabic, a language he picked up from his Lebanese mother, he's an invaluable asset to the CIA and the country. He's a good looking guy, about 45 years old, with a dark complexion and deep brown eyes. He wears his jet-black hair closely cropped. I've heard him say often that he has no time to waste combing his hair. Buster and I have become close-working colleagues as well as good friends over the past few months. He was instrumental in helping to free Ellen from the kidnapping last year. He helped save Ellen's life, and that fact alone makes him my friend.

Although he has an office at 26 Federal Plaza in New York, Buster had been away for a week at CIA headquarters in Langley, Virginia. Barbara gave him a hug, and so did I. Sometimes I feel like he's my brother.

"So here's the story, folks," said Buster. "We've been worried about SAMs for a long time. We've found out that ISIS came into possession of hundreds of them in Iraq. Yesterday's airplane attack leads us to believe that the missile may have come from ISIS. At this point, it's just a hunch, and I don't like to plan based on hunches."

ISIS is an acronym that I've grown to hate. It means the Islamic State in Iraq and Syria. It's also known as ISIL, for the Islamic State in the Levant, the Levant being a region that includes the countries of Iraq, Syria, Eastern Libya, and the Sinai Peninsula of Egypt. Whether you call it ISIS or ISIL, the words *Islamic State* are the most important. It's an attempt by a bunch of terrorist killers to gain a political identity of statehood. The goal is to bring into the world a caliphate, a state run according to the Sharia Laws of Islam, a government that has no pretense toward any democratic institutions. Dhimmis, or subjects, of an Islamic State are just that, subjects, not self-defined individuals in the body politic, but human beings whose lives are controlled by a religious/political philosophy that got its start over 700 years ago.

"What hits me between the eyes," said Barbara, "is that there's little we can do to stop a missile attack on an aircraft. A man hiding in the bushes is just that, a man hiding in the bushes. We can't send an army to sweep every area around an airport before a plane lands or takes off. Buster, your thoughts on the matter?"

"Yes, there is something we can do. Every SAM made or deployed by our armed forces has a tracking device imbedded into its mechanism. Think of it like the tracker in your cell phone. The enemy doesn't know this, or at least we think that's the case."

"Do you mean that we can spot one of these missiles before a plane begins its approach?" I asked.

"That's exactly what I mean, Rick."

"But how can we track every landing or takeoff zone for a missile in the bushes?"

"It will cost a ton of money," said Buster, "but it's what we have to do. The White House is all over this like a blanket. Just as the jihadis put the screws to ground transportation and the cruise ship industry, now they're aiming at a critical part of our economy. Would you want to fly in an airplane that can be knocked out of the sky by a scumbag hiding in the bushes?"

"Do you mean we'll have to sweep every landing and takeoff zone for every plane in the country?" asked Barbara.

"I'm afraid so," said Buster. "Before any plane lands or takes off, a drone will sweep the area to hunt for the tracking device on a possible missile in hiding. American air travel is about to get a lot more expensive—and a lot slower."

"Madam Director, I suggest you turn on the TV," yelled a voice over the intercom.

═╣╠═

"This is Shepard Smith for Fox News, ladies and gentlemen. For our viewers who have just tuned in, I have distressing news. Another aircraft has been shot down by what appears to have been a surface-to-air missile. Delta flight 219 was on its final approach to O'Hare Airport in Chicago when an object was seen streaking toward the plane just moments before it exploded. This announcement comes on the heels of yesterday's report of a United Airlines jet that was shot down as it approached Newark Airport in New Jersey. We're told that the Delta flight carried 237 passengers; and from the view of the wreckage, it's unlikely there are any survivors. In the United Airlines attack yesterday, over 300 died. President Reynolds is scheduled to speak from the White House at 2 p.m. today. We will keep our viewers informed as we receive more information."

# CHAPTER THREE

Captain Jimmy Thompson, the skipper of the *S.S. Cape Orlando*, prepared to enter Baltimore Harbor. The *Orlando* was a small freighter that plied the waters off the east coast of the United States. At 7 a.m., the pilot boat pulled alongside. After the crew secured the boat to the platform, the pilot climbed the ladder and headed toward the bridge to maneuver the vessel into port. As the pilot boat motored away, a Coast Guard patrol boat pulled alongside the *Orlando*. Ever since the events that began on 10/15, every merchant vessel entering an American port required a Coast Guard officer to interview the captain and search the cargo.

"Hi, Jimmy," said the Coast Guard lieutenant as he entered the bridge.

"Good morning, Lieutenant Phil, welcome aboard," said Thompson as he handed a cargo manifest to the officer.

"So what are you hauling today, Jimmy, same old crap?"

"Beats me, Phil. My job is just to drive this thing. Whatever's in the hold is on the manifest. Coffee?"

"No thanks. Let's go to the hold so I can do my checklist."

The two men entered the ship's hold. Lt. Phil carried the manifest attached to a clipboard. He walked the area, randomly comparing items of cargo against what was on the document.

It's tougher to check your groceries out of Costco than to get security clearance for a cargo ship in this port, Thompson thought to himself.

A flatbed trailer truck pulled up next to the ship. The crew loaded two sleds of baking flour onto the truck, along with two dozen 50-gallon drums of cooking oil. The cargo manifest showed that the items originated at a Sysco food company plant in Delaware, and were bound for various supermarkets around Baltimore. Lt. Phil stifled a yawn as he finished his check-off routine.

"Have a good day, Jimmy. See you next time."

After the Coast Guard officer left, a detail of 12 men unloaded 40 sacks covered in plastic from a void space next to the starboard cargo hold. The sacks weren't visible on an inspection of the hold, and their contents were not on the cargo manifest. The men loaded the sacks onto a boat that was tied up on the starboard side of the *Orlando*. The boat pulled away. They then unloaded the same number of sacks from a void on the portside of the ship and carried them onto another boat. Thompson had been given strict orders not to allow the starboard and portside sacks to come near each other.

The boats took their cargo to a residential canal off Baltimore harbor and maneuvered to a dock behind a private house. Each shipment of sacks was unloaded into a different van.

"The operation is completed, Brother Islam," said the first mate.

"Dammit, how many times do I have to tell you not to use my Muslim name? My name is Jimmy Thompson."

After the ship cast off its lines and got underway, Captain Thompson, aka Islam Yamani, removed his prayer rug from the locker in his stateroom and checked his compass for the bearing that faced Mecca.

# CHAPTER FOUR

E llen gave me a shoulder rub as I read *The New York Times.* We were enjoying a quiet Sunday by ourselves.

"I see you're working on my stress reduction list, Rick. You did your yoga this morning, a half hour on the treadmill, and a 20-minute meditation. And last night, when we handled number one, it was just, well, *wow.* I'm proud of you."

She leaned over and kissed my ear as she continued to rub my shoulders.

"Hey, look at this, babe. One of your books, *Enjoy Modern Architecture,* is back on the Best Seller List. Let's go to your favorite restaurant tonight to celebrate. We have to figure out a way to spend all the money you make.

"Holy shit," I almost screamed as I came across an article in the *Times.*

"What, did they mention my book again?"

"Listen to this. A dozen women in a village in Afghanistan came down with dementia. They were all between 25 and 45 years old. This article says that it was extremely fast-acting and that they were in an advanced state of mental deterioration within 48 hours after they first showed symptoms. The authorities are calling it Alzheimer's disease, but they really don't know."

"My God, that's horrible," Ellen said. "Twelve women in one village? What the hell could it possibly be?"

"When something comes from out of left field, it usually means something. It's a dot, a clue. Whenever we say to ourselves, 'that can't possibly be,' it usually means something is going on. But what the hell can this mean?"

# CHAPTER FIVE

Maria Adams, age 37, was appointed Deputy Secretary of State for Middle Eastern Affairs by President Reynolds on January 22. She graduated from Columbia University with a bachelor's degree in history, and received her PhD in Public Policy from Harvard. *The New York Times*, often a harsh critic of President Reynolds' personnel selections, hailed her as "one of the finest, if youngest, experts on Middle Eastern Affairs that the State Department has seen in a long time." Adams had written a book, published by Harvard University Press, entitled *The Middle East: A Crucible for Our Times*.

On February 22, the Senate Foreign Relations Committee convened for a special meeting. Maria Adams was scheduled to testify at 2 p.m. Senator Ross Fenster, Chairman of the Foreign Relations Committee, called the meeting to order at 1:30. Maria Adams was scheduled to meet with Fenster before the meeting, but she wasn't there. Amy Patiston, Adam's assistant, called the deputy secretary on her cell phone.

"Maria, it's Amy. Is everything okay? You're due to testify in about 20 minutes."

"Where?"

"Hey, Maria, you know. You're due to talk in front of the Foreign Relations Committee at two."

"Why?"

"Where are you, Maria?"

"I don't know."

<hr/>

At 4 p.m., Washington D.C. police officer Jerome Langston saw a woman walking barefoot along H Street in Georgetown. The temperature was 25 degrees with a stiff wind. The woman's hair was uncombed and her clothing was disheveled, with her blouse hanging out over her skirt. She wasn't wearing a coat. He approached the woman and asked her name. She said that she didn't know.

"I need backup in front of the Ridge Diner on H Street. I need a female officer backup."

Officer Margie Perez walked up to Langston. She glanced at the disheveled barefoot woman and smiled.

"Why don't we invite our friend for a cup of coffee, Jerry?"

They knew they couldn't arrest the woman for walking barefoot, but she seemed to be in some kind of distress, and it was their job to offer help.

"Do you mind if I ask you for your identification?" said Perez.

"Where's that?"

"It's probably in your pocketbook. Mind if I have a look?"

Her driver's license identified her as Maria Adams, and a card with a photo ID indicated that she was Deputy Secretary of State.

Langston called the desk officer at the police district. Because of the woman's title, he figured this could be a big deal. The district officer called the State Department, and within a few minutes, Amy Patiston showed up.

"Hey, Maria. What's up, hon?"

Adams smiled at Patiston and said nothing.

At 7 p.m. that evening, Maria Adams was admitted to Georgetown University Hospital's mental evaluation unit. The doctors were confused. Even though the woman was only 37 years old, her symptoms indicated severe dementia, mimicking Alzheimer's disease. The doctors were shocked by the suddenness of the symptoms.

# CHAPTER SIX

B uster and I were in Barbara Auletta's office for yet another meeting.

"Rick, I have to ask you something," said Barbara Auletta. "Just before you answered your phone, you cracked up laughing. Were you expecting to hear something funny?"

"Blame it on my wife. Ellen's on a crusade to calm me down. She's worried that I'm starting to burn out, so she came up with a plan to remake Rick Bellamy. One of the items on her list is for me to think of a joke before I answer my phone or turn on the TV. It puts my mind in a good place to hear bad news. I just thought of a Jerry Seinfeld routine before I picked up the phone. I carry a list of his jokes in my wallet."

I showed Barbara and Buster my list of Jerry Seinfeld jokes. I noticed that they scribbled notes.

"That wife of yours is one of the most incredible people I've ever met," said Auletta. "I'd love to convince her to change careers. Imagine having her talents here at the FBI. She'd have to take a 90 percent pay cut, I guess, but her work would be a lot more exciting."

"Well, you'll get to pick her brain a bit in a little while. She's meeting me here for lunch."

"Before we get to the Chicago disaster," said Buster, "I'd like to comment on Ellen. As usual, the woman has hit something right on the head. We all have an obligation to keep our heads screwed on tightly. Our job isn't just to listen to upsetting phone calls and bad news on the TV. Our job is to anticipate and react. Ellen's right. We have to lighten up. Hey, Rick, are you a religious man?"

"Religious?" I said. "Why do you ask?"

"Because you should go to church and get down on your knees and thank God that he sent you a woman like her."

I just smiled.

"To change the subject," I said, "when do you think we'll put into place the missile tracking procedure?"

"The President will speak to the nation at 2 p.m., but don't expect him to announce what I told you about the tracking devices. If we tip our hands, we'll lose a great source of information from any of the jihadis we capture. I expect that he'll put the plan into effect quietly and immediately."

Buster's cell phone went off. Before he answered, he cracked up laughing.

"See, Ellen's plan works," I said to Barbara as Buster picked up his call.

Buster didn't talk, he just listened to the voice on the other end, saying, "I got it, I got it," as he scribbled notes. He hung up and looked at us.

"I notice you're not laughing anymore," I said.

"That was my contact at the FAA. This will soon be all over the news. Get this—90 percent, that's 90-fucking-percent, of all foreign and domestic flight reservations have been cancelled. The jihadis have done it again, this time to air travel. It will be a while before things settle down and we're able to take out the missiles before they fire. For the time being, people are just afraid to fly. Can you blame them?"

———◆+◆———

Barbara's intercom announced, "Mrs. Bellamy is here to see Agent Rick."

Barbara's assistant escorted Ellen to the room. Ellen burst into the office with her usual infectious enthusiasm. "How the hell are you guys?" Ellen said as she hugged me and gave Barbara and Buster a high-five. "Hey, Buster, nice suit. Can you take Rick shopping with you?"

The mood in the room lightened, as usual, because Ellen was around.

# CHAPTER SEVEN

Angela Johnston had just been appointed President of the University of Michigan at the young age of 42. During the seemingly endless rounds of interviews, she impressed the members of the board of trustees with her scholarship, her skills at dealing with squabbling factions, as well as her fundraising talents. She had taken McGloon College, a struggling institution on the verge of bankruptcy, and turned it around, putting its budget in the black and increasing student enrollment by 30 percent in just three years. Having graduated first in her class from Stanford, she went on to receive a PhD from Yale.

"I think we have ourselves a winner," said Jacob Menzies, the chairman of the board of trustees, as he addressed an executive committee meeting. "Angela's not only smart as hell, but she has an amazing ability to bring people together. She picked that little college out of the scrap heap, made it solvent, and turned it into a regional star. As you'll see shortly, Angela is also an excellent public speaker."

The board members filed out of the conference room and into the auditorium, where Angela Johnston would address them as well as 180 faculty members and staff.

Menzies, with a long career in business, government, and academia, knew how to introduce a speaker. After a five-minute introduction, during which Menzies told the assembled all about Johnston's educational credentials as well as her string of successes, he called her to the podium.

"Ladies and gentlemen, the new President of the University of Michigan, Doctor Angela Johnston!"

In keeping with tradition, all of the assembled gave her a standing ovation.

Johnston approached the podium as the applause continued.

"Why is everybody standing?" she said into the microphone.

The audience laughed. Everybody appreciates a little self-deprecating humor at the start of a talk.

"I mean, no shit," Johnston said, "what the hell is this all about?"

A few chuckled, most cleared their throats.

Menzies, trying to reclaim a situation that was spinning into an unknown direction, stepped up to the microphone and tilted it his way.

"I told you folks that we hired a no-nonsense woman. Angela's showing you her tough Brooklyn roots."

She looked at Menzies and said, "And who the fuck are you?"

Almost every attendee in the audience of over 200 people suddenly had an irresistible urge to check their cell phones. Email, weather, ball scores—anything to distract them from what was happening before their eyes.

Johnston held onto the podium with both hands and stared out at the audience. An agonizingly long minute went by. She finally spoke.

"Fuck this, I'm hungry." She walked toward the back of the stage, but was unable to find the opening in the curtain.

Angela Johnston, PhD, newly appointed President of the University of Michigan at age 42, now resides at the Petit Flower Nursing Home in Ann Arbor. She has been diagnosed with severe dementia. One doctor speculated that it might be early-onset Alzheimer's disease, but he had never heard of it acting so quickly. Nor had he seen the disease attack someone so young.

# CHAPTER EIGHT

Ellen and I walked to our favorite lunch place, Chez Amis. The maître d' showed us to our usual table in the back. Like the Carnegie Deli, Chez Amis doesn't take credit cards.

"How much cash do you have?" I asked Ellen.

"Only about 20 dollars."

"I better go to the ATM."

"I'll get it, hon, I'm closer," said Ellen.

After about five minutes, Ellen came back to the table. Her face told me something was wrong. Did we let the account run low? I thought.

"Rick, I forgot my friggin PIN number."

"No problem, honey, I'll use my card."

I retrieved our cash and came back to the table. Ellen wore a frown and fidgeted with her napkin.

"Hey, pickle puss, how about a smile?"

"Rick, I've been using that PIN for years. I use it at least once a week. How the hell could I just forget it?"

"Hey, don't sweat it, hon. With everything you have stored in that pretty head of yours, it's inevitable that a few things will leak out."

"Rick, how many times have you told me I have a memory like an elephant? I don't forget things. I just don't."

"Listen, Ms. Stress Coach. You've been all over me to decompress. Stop getting upset over a little thing. The next time you go to the bank, simply get a new card and a new PIN number. Probably a good idea for security anyway. Here's some cash."

We talked about a new project Ellen was working on. Her new client was a suburban school district in New Jersey. They had plenty of money, thanks to the taxpayers, and they wanted Ellen to design a new state-of-the-art administration building. She made a rough sketch on her notepad to show me.

"This is beautiful, babe, but it looks like a private home, not an administration building."

"Oh shit, I must have gotten it confused with another project."

As we finished lunch, we went over a few chores that we had divvied up between us.

"Hey, hon, don't forget to call Blake."

"Blake?"

"Yeah, the painting contractor. Remember, we want an estimate to repaint our kitchen."

"Oh, yeah, Blake. I must have his phone number. That's Drake, right? D-R-A-K-E?"

"No problem, hon. You have a rich school district to worry about. I'll call Blake."

Ellen was totally overworked, I concluded. Time to think about a vacation.

# CHAPTER NINE

"Rick, it's Barbara. Turn on the TV."

Shit, I thought. I'm getting to hate it whenever somebody says turn on the TV. Wait, I reminded myself as I reached for the index card joke collection in my shirt pocket. As I pressed the remote, I laughed out loud over the latest Jerry Seinfeld gag on my list. I stopped laughing soon.

"Shepard Smith for Fox News, ladies and gentlemen. Law enforcement authorities the world over are bracing for the reaction from Islamic radicals over this week's cover of *Charlie Hebdo*, the French satirical magazine. As you can see from this photo of the *Hebdo* cover, it shows a depiction of the Prophet Muhammad smoking a cigar and holding a martini glass."

It's about time the media started to grow a set of balls, I thought. Gutsy move for Fox to show the explosive cover.

"As you may recall, ladies and gentlemen," Smith continued, "last year a small group of Islamic radicals stormed the *Charlie Hebdo* office in Paris and slaughtered 12 employees of the magazine and wounded 11. That incident was in protest of yet another cartoon depiction of the Prophet. Our bureau in Paris reports that at least 20 cars have been overturned and set on fire. I'm now going to show you live news feeds from major capitals around the world."

Smith and his staff showed scene after scene of worldwide mayhem. Police in riot gear fired tear gas at seemingly endless numbers of rioters.

Barbara Auletta and Buster walked into my office.

"This is what I've been worried about, guys," Barbara said. "I've been worried, but I can't say I haven't expected it—the backlash."

As Barbara said that, Shepard Smith was showing scenes of mosques on fire and counter-demonstrators in pitched battle with the radicals. Cars, buses, and various other unidentifiable vehicles blazed on the streets.

"Every time I've turned on the TV in the past few months," Barbara said, "I think we've finally hit a flash point, a point of no return, a point where radical Islam and the West clashes and doesn't stop clashing."

"We *have* reached that point," said Buster, "but not this morning. We hit that point when President Reynolds realized the obvious and shared it with the world in his famous speech a few months ago. He announced that World War III had begun, and he was right. What we're seeing on TV is just a spontaneous tantrum of the 'Brotherhood of the Offended,' just another way to vent hatred against the West."

"Brotherhood of the Offended?" said Barbara. "How poetic, Buster."

"Yeah, poetic but accurate, Barbara," I said. "Buster nailed it. We're dealing with people who take a lusty thrill in venting anger over perceived slights. How many times have you read about some Islamic group at an American university claiming that they were insulted by a public display of Christianity or Judaism, something really offensive like a nativity scene in front of a dormitory?

Some universities refuse to serve pork or bacon in their cafeterias. It's almost like radical Muslims consider it a successful day when they've managed to be insulted by somebody, somewhere. Hey, I don't applaud *Charlie Hebdo* for what it does—insult people. But I love the fact that free societies allow satirical magazines to say it. The *Charlie Hebdo*s and *Mad Magazine*s of the world aren't about to stop hurling insults, or even simple jokes. And what Buster calls the Brotherhood of the Offended will be ready to strike out and kill people as a result."

Buster's phone went off. He didn't stop to laugh at his list of jokes.

When Buster got off the phone, his face was pale.

"That was CIA Director Carlini. He talked about the surface-to-air missile attacks, and it just got worse. So far, we've seen attacks with light shoulder-mounted SAMs, useful for firing at a plane landing or taking off, but we've just found out that ISIS has captured a large cache of heavy-duty SAMs, including Patriot missiles. They're not as easy to conceal as a shoulder-mounted weapon, but that doesn't matter. These things have a range of over 90 miles, and can shoot down a plane at cruising altitude, not just when it's landing or taking off. So our tracking devices are useless. We came up with the idea to have drone surveillance of takeoff and landing zones, but that no longer means anything with the big stuff. A truck can hide in the woods and fire a missile at a plane 90 miles away.

"I remember my father telling me about his Marine experience in Viet Nam. The plane carrying military personnel into the country would fly at a high altitude and then go into a steep dive as it approached Tan Son Nhat Airport, the big American base. The purpose was to avoid SAMs. And that was in the 1960s. This front of the war isn't going away any time soon. It's already had a huge impact on the aviation industry—90 percent cancellations."

"So what's next?" I said. I figured I'd ask a stupid question to ease the tension in the room.

"I'm afraid to tell you guys what's next," said Director Auletta. "You're not going to like it."

# CHAPTER TEN

On April 3, United Airlines flight 439 was en route from Bermuda to Logan Airport in Boston, flying off the coast of New Jersey. The flight attendants busied themselves serving a mid-flight snack.

A tractor trailer with the logo "Key Foods" painted on its sides lumbered into a wooded area of a state park in southern New Jersey. Two men got out of the vehicle and opened the rear doors. Inside was a MIM-104 Patriot Missile launcher. The men wheeled a heavy-duty ramp to the end of the trailer, and the Patriot vehicle was slowly lowered to the ground with an electric winch.

A state police car pulled up to the truck and the officer shouted to the men, "This park is closed until May first. Can't you people read the sign?"

One of the men raised his AK-47 and fired a short burst at the cop, killing him instantly.

The Patriot missile struck Flight 439 in mid-fuselage, causing it to erupt in a fireball. The plane, in thousands of parts, fell to the ocean, along with the remains of 273 passengers and crew.

〜✝〜

## Delta and United Airlines Declare Bankruptcy

*The New York Times*
By Randolph Cummings
Within hours of the latest surface-to-air missile attack on an American plane, United Flight 439 from Bermuda to Boston, both United and Delta Airlines have declared bankruptcy. The latest missile attack was different from previous incidents, in that the missile used to strike the United flight was long-range. It struck the jet as it flew at an altitude of 30,000 feet. The FAA, in conjunction with the United States Air Force, had instituted a policy of drone surveillance of landing and takeoff zones for every arriving and departing flight, a policy undertaken at enormous expense and that was responsible for snarled traffic and huge flight delays. The purpose behind the surveillance policy was for an unmanned drone to detect a missile launcher's location and then attack it.

Yesterday's United disaster, however, has put a new and startling face on the nation's air travel.

According to Ken Williams, CEO of United, "The use of heavy-duty long-range missiles creates a brand new ballgame. Simply put, with the enemy deploying long-range SAMs, no aircraft is safe, whether it's landing, taking off, or simply cruising at high altitude."

When asked why United had chosen to seek bankruptcy, Williams stated, "The airline industry, when you boil it down to essentials, isn't complicated. We sell seats. No seat sales, no revenue. No revenue, no profit. Our sales are off 90 percent since the surface-to-air missile crisis began a few weeks ago. Our industry has had to change overnight."

According to Elizabeth Jones, Secretary of Transportation, "These attacks have caused the most dramatic reversal of an industry that the country, actually the world, has ever seen."

Air France, Alitalia, Lufthansa, and British Airways have all reported similar historic decreases in ticket reservations.

A White House spokesman, who asked not to be named because of the sensitive nature of the problem, said, "For the near future, the world is grounded. Both the Air Force and civilian aviation leaders are feverishly working on plans to equip all commercial aircraft with anti-missile defenses. The cost will be enormous and the effectiveness, with our current state of technology, cannot be guaranteed."

# CHAPTER ELEVEN

John and Dolores Shankman, both in their mid-60s, had recently retired from Oracle Corporation with comfortable pensions. They had always discussed a dream vacation—a train trip through the Canadian Rockies. They carefully planned their trip for April, a time when spring was getting its bloom on.

They boarded the Royal Canadian Pacific train in Vancouver, British Columbia. The train would take them through the Canadian Rockies to Banff, where they would meet their son and daughter-in-law and their three grandchildren.

The train had just rolled onto a bridge a few miles outside of Calgary.

A man seated on a rock outcropping 500 feet from the bridge pressed his detonator button and dived behind a boulder. A 40-pound bag of the explosive Tannerite blasted away the middle of the bridge and sent the train in an accordion-like spiral of death to the valley floor 300 feet below, along with its 350 passengers. No one survived. The man had purchased the Tannerite, consisting of ammonium nitrate and aluminum powder, at a nearby sporting goods store. He paid cash.

# CHAPTER TWELVE

Regina Townsend, age 38, became the first woman president of the New York Stock Exchange on March 11. Long a "Wall Street Darling," according to *Forbes*, Townsend was also a recognized face in living rooms across America. Because of her wit, her wry sense of humor, and her piercing intellect, she was a favorite of news anchors and talk show hosts across the nation.

Townsend graduated from Duke University with a degree in economics. She then went on to get an MBA from the Wharton Business School of the University of Pennsylvania, and a law degree from Yale. She became a partner at Goldman Sachs at the age of 35. Nobody questioned her credentials or background when her Stock Exchange presidency was announced. "The New York Stock Exchange," the *Wall Street Journal* gushed, "may have just found the leader it desperately needs."

Townsend was on Fox Business News being interviewed by Neil Cavuto.

"Welcome to my show, *Your World*, Regina, and thank you for joining us." They were longtime friends, and Cavuto always used her first name. "You have your work cut out for you, Regina. The New York Stock Exchange is under a ton of pressure from the on-line trading industry. Please tell our audience some of your ideas going forward."

"I'm sorry. What did you say?" Townsend said, looking at Cavuto with a wrinkled brow.

"I'd just like you to give us some of your ideas for bringing the New York Stock Exchange back to its former glory."

"Glory me, I don't know."

"Come on, Regina," said Cavuto with a smile, "we've known each other for a long time. Don't be so cagey. Tell our viewers some of your ideas."

"Can I have a glass of water?"

"Hey, you can have a beer if it will open you up," Cavuto joked.

"Yes, a beer would be nice. Do I know you?"

Cavuto put his right hand to his earpiece as his producer told him they were cutting to an unscheduled commercial break. The producer walked next to Cavuto.

"Regina, we're off the air on a break. Is everything okay? Talk to me, my friend. You seem like you're upset about something. Should we cut the interview short? I can have you back at another time."

"Who are you? Please tell me why I'm here."

Regina Townsend broke down sobbing. The producer told a man in the control booth to bring on the next guest. When the commercial break ended, Cavuto told his listeners that Townsend was called away on sudden business.

That evening, Regina Townsend, age 38, was taken to Bellevue Hospital. Her husband waited for her at the entrance. She didn't recognize him. She underwent a battery of mental exams, and three days later was transferred to a nursing home. Her diagnosis was severe sudden-onset dementia.

# CHAPTER THIRTEEN

Barbara Auletta clicked on the TV as her assistant suggested over the intercom. Auletta had called the meeting. Besides Buster and me, Bennie Weinberg and my former partner Zeke Martin were there.

Dr. Benjamin Weinberg, a psychiatrist and detective with the NYPD, was on loan to the FBI. Bennie is nationally famous for his skills in detecting lies, especially from people on the witness stand. Bennie, age 45, is a short man at 5'8," slightly overweight, and has a bald spot on the top of his head. After he graduated from Harvard Medical School, Bennie served as a combat physician with the 82nd Airborne Division and served in Afghanistan. After he mustered out, Bennie went on to complete his residency in psychiatry. Along with his academic credentials, Ben is an expert marksman. He's popular with prosecutors across the country. His nickname, which he hates, is Bennie the Bullshit Detector. Although his academic credentials would lead you to think he'd come across as an intellectual, Bennie opts for the tough demeanor of a cop. His sentences are copiously sprinkled with f-bombs. He's also a good friend.

Barbara hit the remote so fast I didn't have time to read a Seinfeld joke, my usual routine before watching anything on television.

Fox News anchor Gretchen Carlson was reporting the wreck of a Royal Canadian Pacific train outside of Calgary, Canada.

"It was clearly a deliberate act, from what we've learned in the past few minutes," said Carlson. "Four eyewitnesses reported seeing a massive explosion in the middle of a bridge just as the train approached it. The train, carrying 350 passengers, plunged 300 feet to the valley below. Emergency crews are on the scene, but it's doubtful there are any survivors."

Somehow, this news report seemed like an apt way to start the meeting of the FBI's New York Counterterrorism Unit.

Auletta clicked off the TV and began to discuss our agenda, which was the surface-to-air missile crisis.

"Excuse me," said Bennie, "but I have an observation. We just heard about a horrible train wreck that killed 350 people and which is most likely terror related. It's definitely an intentional act—a train bridge was blown up. And I want us all to notice something, including me. We haven't even mentioned it. A train disaster would once consume our entire attention, but now we don't even give it a thought. We're becoming numb, folks, fucking numb. I just want to raise a flag of caution, and I'm waving it in front of my own face as well. We can't abandon our emotions. We need them. To the extent we abandon our emotions is the extent to which we'll become like robots, and the enemy is anything but."

"Bennie," said Auletta, "God bless you, and thank you for your gentle criticism. You're absolutely right. We've talked a lot about keeping our emotions under control with the constant barrage of horror, but there's a big difference between controlling emotions and forgetting that we have them."

We all applauded. It seemed like a strange thing to applaud, but I think Bennie and Barbara both told us something that we needed to hear.

"And speaking of emotions," Barbara said, "I have an announcement that will get us all emotional. I don't think you're going to like what I have to tell you."

Barbara stood and walked to the front of the room. She knows how to get attention and how to position herself when she needs to say something important.

"What I'm about to tell you guys is, at this point, a rumor," Barbara said, "but it's a rumor that was passed to me by Sarah Watson, Director of the FBI. She said it came as a high-level leak from the White House, and whenever that happens, somebody is usually running something up the flagpole to assess public opinion."

"So it's actually more than a rumor," I said, "it's an informal survey."

"Yes, it is, Rick, and I'll get right to the point. President Reynolds is toying with the idea of suspending the right of *habeas corpus*, the right to a hearing on the issue of unlawful detainment. Gentlemen, the president is considering martial law."

She looked at her notes.

"According to Article 1, Section 9 of the United States Constitution, 'The Privilege of the Writ of *Habeas Corpus* shall not be suspended, unless when in Cases of Rebellion or Invasion, the Public Safety may require it.' Hey, is it a stretch for someone to argue that we're under 'invasion,' and that 'the public safety may require' a suspension of *habeas corpus*?"

"Oh my God," said Buster, "this could lead to a fucking dictatorship. I don't want to credit those sand monkeys with far-sighted planning, but could this be what 10/15 and all the shit since then has been all about? Put so much pressure on us that the president concludes that 'public safety may require' an abandonment of our most basic constitutional right? If they pull that one off, they've gone a long way to changing the basic structure of American society. Will Sharia Law look so bad next to a system of martial law?"

"The four of us represent law enforcement and intelligence," I said. "Without *habeas corpus,* you can replace us with drones and robots. I hope to hell Sarah Watson from the FBI and Bill Carlini at CIA try to talk some sense into his head."

"As I told you guys when I made this announcement," said Barbara, "at this point, it's a rumor; but it's a rumor with a purpose, and that purpose is to gauge public response. Well the response from the four of us appears to be unanimous—the idea sucks. I can tell you that Sarah Watson feels that way too."

"I'm sure you can count on Director Carlini to be on the side of daylight," said Buster.

"Okay, guys, but here's what worries me," I said, "and I know it worries you too. With every plane or train that gets blown up, for every cruise ship that sinks, for every random act of explosive terror, the public gets more and more fed up. That's how Stalin held power. He kept things peaceful on the home front by murdering the opposition. People were willing to look the other way because he made their lives relatively peaceful. That's the way any dictator works, which is why we studied in political science that a dictatorship is the most efficient form of government. It may be the worst, but it's the most efficient. Mark my words, guys, there may come a tipping point when the American people are going to scream for law enforcement to 'lock 'em up' and ask questions later. That's exactly what a country looks like without a right to *habeas corpus,* except there's nobody to ask questions, even later."

"At this point," Buster said, "I'd say the jihadis are ahead."

"I have something important to show you guys," I said.

I walked over to the corner of the office and lifted a 40-pound box.

"I've been meaning to ask you what that is, Rick," said Barbara.

"This small box," I said as I held it up, "has enough explosive power in it to blow up a house."

"How the hell did you get that stuff in here?" said Barbara.

"It was quite simple. I ordered it online from Dick's Sporting Goods Store in New Rochelle, and had it delivered here. I used my private credit card. Security stopped the UPS driver, and let him through when they saw it was addressed to me. I also had the same-sized box delivered to my apartment. No questions. The doorman just held it for me in the lobby."

"What the hell is it?" asked Buster.

"It's called Tannerite, and it's perfectly legal. It's used by gun sportsmen to blow up targets."

"Wait, Rick, how the hell can it be legal if it's explosive?"

"It's a loophole, Barbara. The contents of this box are not classified as explosives—yet. The shipment includes containers of ammonium nitrate along with containers of aluminum powder. Mix them together following the simple instructions and you have one hell of a bomb. You may remember that *60 Minutes* did a show on this a few months ago. They quoted a spokesman for Tannerite Sports LLC, the people who make the stuff. 'No additional regulations are needed beyond current laws because the product is safe when used correctly,' the guy said, and 'the only injuries that have ever happened were results from the shooter misusing the product.' The man then added, 'Only girly-men want to regulate Tannerite Rifle Targets.' "

"Well count me in as a 'girlie man,' " said Buster. "This is fucking ridiculous. You can buy explosives by mail order with no questions asked? I remember that ammonium nitrate, which is also used to make fertilizer, was the main ingredient in the bomb that took down the Murrah Federal Building in Oklahoma City back in 1995. But with this Tannerite crap, a jihadi doesn't even have to know about bomb making. Just mix and detonate."

"I've been following up on the investigation of the bombings since 10/15," I said. "The forensic reports all showed traces of ammonium nitrate and aluminum powder. Nobody connected the dots to discover that the shit is commercially available."

"So let me get this straight," said Barbara. "All a lone-wolf jihadi has to do is go to a sporting goods store, take out his cash, and walk out of the place with bomb materials."

"That's pretty much it, Barbara. There's all sorts of political noise about banning the stuff, but it won't do much good. You'll still be able to buy ammonium nitrate and aluminum powder separately and make your own bomb, just without the trademark Tannerite. Blowing things up has gotten a lot simpler."

Barbara cleared her throat and took a sip of water.

"Rick, you've managed to scare the hell out of us this morning with this Tannerite stuff. But besides that and the possibility of martial law, there's another important thing I want to cover this morning. I'm happy to see that our friend Zeke Martin, Rick's former partner, is here with us. Zeke's been transferred to FBI headquarters in D.C. because of his amazing handling of our massive database. Zeke doesn't need a database, he *is* a database. Zeke's going to give us a summary of everything that's happened since 10/15. He's also prepared a detailed handout for each of us."

Zeke walked to the head of the room. We all applauded, especially me. I miss him as a partner but I recognize that his talents are needed at the top. I raised my hand and asked Barbara if I could say a few words of introduction for my former partner.

"You all know Zeke, but I'm not sure how well," I said. "Let me tell you a few things about this guy. After he graduated from the University of Michigan, where he was a runner-up All American wide receiver, he was tapped by the New York Jets as a first-round draft pick. Zeke could have been a millionaire professional athlete and, in this media market, he would have also made a bundle on

TV selling stuff with his handsome face. But no, he chose to serve his country instead. After serving with the Army in Afghanistan, he went to law school. Then he wrote a book that hit *The New York Times* Best Seller List, *Running for Glory*, a cautionary tale about the physical dangers of college and pro football. After that, he could have capitalized on his celebrity status, but he chose instead to continue to serve his country, now with the FBI. Zeke is one of the best people we have, and we should all be proud to serve with him."

That brought another round of applause.

"Zeke, please talk to us."

"After an introduction like that, Rick, I can't wait to hear myself. I remember Rick and I sitting in Barbara's office on October 15 when the shit hit the fan. Rick's office had just been wrecked by a bomb that blew up downstairs, and Barbara was sitting there with a cold compress against her head wound. We were shocked at what occurred, but we had no idea what would happen in the following months. Train wrecks, building explosions, two sunken cruise ships, two college football stadium attacks, and of course, the biggest terror spectacular to date, the Super Bowl. Bennie is absolutely right—we're becoming numb, emotionally drained, but we can't let that happen.

"FBI Director Watson asked me to deliver a message to you folks. As the key team in the FBI's counterterrorism task force, the country looks to you. It's as if Director Watson heard what Bennie said a few minutes ago. She wants us all to keep our emotions in check, but not to forget that we have them. It's only by keeping in touch with our emotions that we'll be able to recognize the difference between us and the barbarians who want to kill us. My job is to keep you all up to date about our findings at headquarters. Without your input, our records would be empty. I want you all to know I'm honored to serve with you."

Zeke's a good man. I'm glad he's on our side. Both he and Bennie, as well as Barbara, made damn good points about our emotions.

My emotions would soon be tried to the breaking point.

# CHAPTER FOURTEEN

The *USS Gideon Welles,* an Ohio Class nuclear ballistic missile submarine, was on patrol in the North Atlantic off Norway under 400 feet of water. The *Welles,* named after the Secretary of the Navy in the Lincoln administration, was the second Navy vessel to carry the name. The first was a destroyer that was decommissioned in 1940.

In addition to its complement of Mark 48 torpedoes, the *Welles* carried 24 Trident nuclear ballistic missiles.

Lieutenant Commander Roger McCue, the weapons officer, lodged a chair under the door handle of his stateroom to ensure that he wouldn't be interrupted. He reached into his locker and took out his prayer rug. Checking the compass on the bulkhead, he arranged the rug to face Mecca so that he could perform his evening prayers.

After he finished praying, McCue placed his rug back into his locker and removed the chair from underneath the door handle. McCue, also known to a select few people as Ali Shabana, put on his uniform and headed to his watch station in "Sherwood Forest," the compartment on the sub that held the ballistic missiles.

While in port, McCue, over a period of weeks, lugged small bags of plastic explosives, the same quantity that had blown open the hull of the *USS Cole* in October 2000. Every time he was on watch, McCue would lower the bags into a void between the inner and outer hull. Each bag was equipped with a remote control firing mechanism.

He saluted Lieutenant Commander Douglas Pittman, the officer he was about to relieve. After they went over the log of the watch, Pittman left the compartment.

He had just opened a hatch leading to the void when Lt. Juan Cordoba, the assistant watch officer, approached him and said, "What the hell?"

McCue removed his pistol from his belt and shot Cordoba through the chest.

"Allahu Akbar," he chanted three times before he pressed the detonator button.

The blast ripped through the hull of the *Welles*, causing an implosion as the seawater under 400 feet of pressure roared in to fill the void.

The *USS Gideon Welles*, with its crew of 140 men, sank to the bottom of the ocean in thousands of pieces, including the remnants of the nuclear missiles.

# CHAPTER FIFTEEN

I got home later than usual, about 8 p.m. It was great having Ellen stop by the office yesterday. I think Barbara Auletta is serious about trying to recruit her into the FBI, not that Ellen would ever go for the idea.

Ellen usually meets me at the door, but I saw that she was sitting in the den. The TV was off.

"Hey, hon, gimme a kiss," I said as I sat next to her.

We kissed, but it wasn't our usual smooch. The look on Ellen's face told me that she was upset about something. No smile, not a word. She didn't even look at me.

"Everything okay, honey?" I asked. "You're not still worried about forgetting your bank PIN are you?"

"What PIN?"

Ever since I've known Ellen, her response when seeing me always began with a smile. But she wasn't smiling. She sat upright on the couch with her hands clasped together in her lap. I reached over and stroked her face. She continued to look straight ahead at the blank TV screen.

"I'm going to change into jeans, honey" I said. "I'll be right back."

"My name is Ellen."

I went into our bedroom to change. I had no idea what the hell was going on. All I knew was that my heart was pounding like a drum. After I changed into jeans and a sweatshirt, I sat down again next to Ellen. Her hands remained in her lap and she stared at the blank TV screen. Still no smile.

"Hey, honey, tell me what's new with that big school project you're working on."

Ellen always gets excited about big new projects, so I figured my question would cheer her up.

"I don't go to school."

My cell phone buzzed, telling me that I had a text message. Before I tapped on the message, I cracked up, thinking about a Jerry Seinfeld joke as per Ellen's de-stressing plan for me. I saw that it was Buster, just texting me a message that he'd be a half-hour late for our meeting the next day.

"Hey, babe, did you notice? I just did my Jerry Seinfeld routine?"

"Who's Jerry Seinfeld?"

<hr/>

Something was wrong. Something was crazy wrong.

When Ellen and I went to bed, I began one of the worst nights of my life. I hardly slept at all. After we crawled under the covers, I put my arm across Ellen and pulled her closer to me, something I do so often it's almost a ritual.

Ellen turned her face toward the wall and said, "Why are you doing that?"

At about 2 a.m., Ellen got out of bed. Five minutes went by, then ten. I got up and put on my robe. I walked into the guest bedroom to see if she was there. Sometimes, when one of us couldn't sleep, we'd go to the guest room so as not to keep each other awake. She wasn't there.

I went into the darkened den and turned on the light, expecting to see her asleep on the couch. She sat, just as she did when I got home, upright on the couch, hands in her lap, staring at the blank TV screen. She didn't seem to notice that I turned on the light.

I sat next to her and put my hand on her leg. She moved my hand from her thigh and rested it on the couch between us.

"Hey, honey, talk to me. We never keep anything from each other. What's wrong, and don't tell me nothing. Is there a problem at the office?"

"Office?"

"Yeah, office. Is something wrong at the office?"

"What office?"

"You know, the office you go to, your architectural firm."

"I work here. What do I do?"

"Why don't you lie down, honey? You need some sleep. You can stay on the couch if you want. I'll get you a comforter."

She just nodded and said, "My name is Ellen."

# CHAPTER SIXTEEN

My alarm went off at 5:30 a.m., my usual waking time. One of the more enjoyable events in life is awakening from a nightmare, only to realize it was just a dream. But it wasn't a bad dream, it was real. I woke up in the middle of a nightmare that wouldn't go away.

I went into the den, where Ellen was finally asleep on the couch. She heard me and opened her eyes. I went to kiss her, but she turned her face.

"I'll put on some coffee, hon."

"My name is Ellen."

Ellen didn't want to eat, but I convinced her to have some cereal with raisins. We sat at the kitchen table. She stared at the opposite wall.

"Do you have anything pressing at the office, Ellen? I thought maybe you and I could take a day off." No way in hell was I about to let her out of my sight.

"Office? What office?"

"You know, Whitney, Cox, and Bellamy. Hey, babe, you're now a big-time named partner."

"Who's my partner?"

I cleared the dishes from the table. I was having the same feeling in my stomach that I get when someone tells me about another terrorist attack.

"I have some phone calls to make, honey. Why don't you sit in the den and watch some TV? I can play that *Forest Gump* video that you love."

"I don't like forests."

"You'll like this one." Something told me that she shouldn't watch any upsetting news reports.

"Whitney, Cox, and, Bellamy," the receptionist said.

"Hi, Joan, it's Rick Bellamy. Is Phil Whitney there?"

"Hi, Rick, it's Phil. Is everything okay?"

"Phil, Ellen can't make it in today. She's feeling under the weather."

"That's why I just asked you if everything is okay, Rick. Yesterday, Ellen seemed, I don't know, not herself. She kept forgetting a lot of things. Maybe you two should take a vacation. You've both been under a lot of stress."

"I may take you up on that, Phil. I'll call you later."

I then texted Barbara Auletta to let her know I'd be working from home today.

⊷⊶

"Ben Weinberg here."

"Bennie, it's Rick. I don't know what you have on your schedule, but I need you to have lunch at my place today."

"You *need* me to have lunch?"

"Yes, Ben, need is the word."

"Rick, what's wrong?"

"It's Ellen, Bennie. She's acting strangely. Something's wrong. I don't want to say more than that. I want you to see for yourself."

Bennie Weinberg is a good friend and a brilliant shrink. He's also a guy who's there when you need him. And I needed him.

⊷ ⊶

Bennie is one of Ellen's favorite people. We often have dinner with Ben and his wife, Maggie. Both Bennie and Ellen share a love of opera, something I'm working on. They also have similar senses of humor. I couldn't wait for him to show up. If anybody can snap Ellen out of this crap, it's Bennie.

Ben rang the bell promptly at 12:15. He walked in carrying a bouquet of flowers. I led him into the den, where Ellen sat.

"Hello, beautiful. These are for you to celebrate your making partner at the firm."

He leaned over to kiss her. She stared at the blank TV.

"Who are you?" Ellen asked Bennie.

"Oh, let's just say that I'm an old friend. You can call me Bennie."

"Hello, Lennie," Ellen said as she stared straight ahead.

"I'm writing a book," politely lied Dr. Bullshit Detector, "and Rick says that you can help me."

"I don't know how to write a book," said Ellen, her hands planted firmly on her lap.

"Well according to *The New York Times* Best Seller List, it seems that you do know quite well how to write books. But don't worry about that, sweetie. I just have a few questions."

"My name is Ellen, not sweetie."

"Sure thing, Ellen. Would you please tell me the name of the firm where you work?"

"Firm? What firm?"

"The architectural firm where you just became a named partner."

"I don't know."

"Did you ever hear of Whitney, Cox, and Bellamy?"

"Are they on television?"

"Is Bellamy your last name?"

"My name is Ellen."

"Do you remember *my* name?"

"George."

Ellen's hands were no longer clasped together on her lap, but were gesturing and fidgeting like crazy. She began to perspire.

"Hey, Ellen, if you don't mind me saying so, you look tired. Did you get much sleep last night?"

"I don't know. I wasn't here."

"Ellen, I'm going to go to the kitchen and pour myself a cup of coffee. Can I get you one?"

"Why?"

"I'll be right back, Ellen. Rick, can you help me with the coffee?"

Bennie and I walked into the kitchen.

"I'm going to give her a mild sedative, Rick. She's in a high state of agitation. It'll knock her out shortly. Then you and I can talk."

Ellen was fast asleep in the guest bedroom at the other end of the apartment. Bennie sat across from me in the den. We dined on sandwiches that I had delivered. I took one bite and put mine down.

"Rick, I may be a psychiatrist, but you're one of the smartest guys I know. Before I say anything, first tell me what *you* think is going on."

"I can't believe I'm about to say this, Ben, but from my experience in life, it almost seems like Ellen is showing signs of Alzheimer's disease. But that's impossible. Just two days ago, Ellen—good old Ellen—was in my office, talking and joking with Barbara and Buster. We then had a great lunch. The only negative thing about lunch was that she forgot her bank PIN number and was pretty upset about it. Just a few days ago, Ellen laid out a detailed plan for me to cope with the stress of my job. Only days ago, Ellen was concerned about *my* mental health. And now she's acting like a fucking zombie."

"Rick, you and I aren't just colleagues, we're friends. You stood by Ellen when she was kidnapped a few months ago, and I stood by you. I'm supposed to be a dispassionate professional and look at this shit clinically, but I admit that I'm upset, really upset. You hit it on the head. The symptoms we're seeing are classic signs of dementia, like we see in Alzheimer's patients. You saw the first indication when she forgot her PIN number. That can happen to anybody, but under the circumstances, I think it was an early marker. The disease isn't a specialty of mine, but I do know a lot about it. Based on what you told me and what I've just seen, I gotta say I'm mystified. Yes, Alzheimer's can act fast, but the speed is measured in *months* and *years*, not fucking hours. And, my God, I've read about it hitting younger people, but 38? That's rare."

"Bennie, is there anything we can do?"

Bennie got up and walked into the kitchen. He splashed cold water on his face and dried off with a couple of paper towels. He walked back into the den, looking sad.

"You're aware, Rick, that there's no cure for Alzheimer's. It isn't just dementia, but a disease that manifests itself physically. Plaque actually forms on the surface of the brain, along with twisted fibers called tangles. And the disease eventually kills the victim. But hey, I'm going to hold out some hope here. Because of her age, and because it happened so fast, I'm thinking that we may be looking at something completely different."

"So what's next, Ben? Please don't tell me that I'm going to have to institutionalize Ellen, and that she's going to die soon. Please don't fucking tell me that, Bennie."

I started to cry, and I didn't give a shit. The center of my life was disappearing from me.

"Here's what I will tell you, Rick. A guy named Harry Noonan is the absolute maven on the subject of Alzheimer's. We were classmates at Harvard Medical School. He's a good friend of mine, and he's located right here in Manhattan. He's affiliated with Columbia Presbyterian."

Bennie placed a call to Dr. Harry Noonan. He explained to his friend what his findings were.

"Harry will be here within the hour, Rick. He wants to see Ellen himself. Meanwhile, you have some preparations to make. Here's the name of an excellent visiting nurse who I've worked with, Olga Burns. You can't leave Ellen alone, obviously. Olga has a lot of experience with dementia patients. Also, you need to get a combination lock that secures the door. The last thing you want is for Ellen to start wandering."

My mind swam as I contemplated what Bennie had just said. Two days ago, I had lunch with my Ellen, the smart, witty Ellen. Now, two days later, I have to be concerned about her wandering off.

# CHAPTER SEVENTEEN

At 2:30, the doorbell rang, and it was Dr. Harry Noonan. He was short and wiry, with a burst of red hair. He had a nervous energy about him that set my nerves on edge. He and Bennie hugged, obviously old friends.

We told Dr. Harry the story of the past 48 hours in the life of Ellen Bellamy. He took notes as we spoke.

"Bennie, it's amazing that you called me when you did. I've just returned from an Alzheimer's conference in Albuquerque. It was the most ground-shaking meeting I've ever attended. There's an article about it in today's *Times*. Make sure you read it."

"Did you see or hear anything about the situation that Ellen Bellamy faces?" asked Bennie.

"Yes, Ben, and I'm about to blow your mind just like mine was blown. The keynote speaker was an epidemiologist named Frank Buchannan who keeps a huge database of dementia patients, their symptoms, history, and the timing of the disease. To get to the main point, the world of Alzheimer's and dementia has changed in the past 12 months, changed radically. According to Buchannan's database, there's been a large increase in Alzheimer's diagnoses in the past year. Not only have the diagnoses skyrocketed, but the patient profiles are shocking as hell. Cases of early-onset dementia have shot off the charts. Rick's wife, Ellen, at age 38, certainly qualifies as an early-onset victim.

"Last year, we expected to see about 490,000 new cases of dementia. Instead, we found that the new cases reported were over 500,000. If the numbers hold as projected, we'll see close to 600,000 cases this year. Now a significant part of that increase is because of the aging baby boomer population, but nothing can explain the dramatic surge in early-onset cases. Right now the surge is in the hundreds, but the projection for the future is staggering. And get this: of those diagnosed as early-onset, 50 percent are under the age of 40. And they're all women. Every blessed one of them are women, young women. Something strange is going on, something we're all trying to come to grips with."

"Doctor Noonan—"

"Please call me Harry."

"Harry, did you read that *New York Times* article about 12 women in a small village in Afghanistan coming down with apparent Alzheimer's symptoms?"

"Yes, Rick, I read the article. The reporter interviewed me for background material. I've been invited by the Afghan government to consult with them, and I'm going there next week."

"Is there anything about all of this that lines up with what you know about Ellen, Harry?"

"It's the speed, Rick. Ellen is not the only person I've heard about coming down with full-blown dementia in a couple of days. But hey, hold on. Here's the most important thing, at least many of us think it is. I'm an expert in Alzheimer's, maybe the nation's leading expert, but my colleagues and I are beginning to think we may be dealing with something entirely different."

"Harry," said Bennie, "are you saying that this disease you're looking at may not be Alzheimer's?"

"Yes, that's what I'm saying. The symptoms mimic Alzheimer's exactly, but we have some flags that have thrown off our thinking. As you probably know, a diagnosis of Alzheimer's can now be done with an MRI, but a definitive diagnosis is done after the fact, by autopsy. The plaque and tangles on the brain are visible on the examining table. At this point, Buchannan has estimated that about 600 women have come down with this thing in the past year. Ten have died and autopsies were performed. Not one of the autopsies confirmed the classic physical manifestation of Alzheimer's—*not one*. A colleague of mine is working on a paper, and she's asked me to review it before publication. She makes a strong case that this disease we're looking at may be some kind of virus or a bacteria, transmittable in the environment."

"Hey, guys, I'm no doctor," I said, "and I think I know the answer to the question I'm about to ask, but can the disease be treated?"

"Rick," said Dr. Harry, "the problem is we don't know what this disease is yet; and therefore, we don't have a treatment protocol in place. We know that genetics plays a big role in traditional Alzheimer's. I want to ask you some questions, Rick, even though we don't know just yet what we're dealing with. Is there any history in your wife's family of dementia?"

"Ellen comes from a close-knit family and I've met every one of them. Her folks are in their 60s and both are sharp as hell. Her grandparents are both alive and in their 80s. They play chess regularly. Her grandfather always beats me, and I'm pretty good. No, I don't know of any dementia in Ellen's family."

"May I see Mrs. Bellamy, please?"

I'd just remembered something, something that should give Harry a better understanding of Ellen than stories from me and Bennie. I picked up my iPad.

"Here's a video I took of Ellen—*three days ago*—at an architectural conference." There was my Ellen, in front to a crowd of 5,000 other architects, giving an articulate, witty, and detailed explanation of a new building design. She had the audience in the palm of her hand.

Harry looked at me. "Three days ago?"

I nodded.

We took Harry into Ellen's room. She had just woken up, still groggy from the sedative that Bennie gave her.

"What do you people want?" she said. "And who the hell are you?" Ellen looked at me when she said that.

Oh, my God. She didn't recognize me.

# CHAPTER EIGHTEEN

Olga Burns rang the doorbell at 8 a.m. the next morning. I had gone through another sleepless night, checking on Ellen every half-hour. Olga was a tall, heavy-set woman with a ready smile. I figured she was about 45 years old. She spoke with a slight Ukrainian accent. As Bennie told me, it was easy to like and trust this woman.

"So, Mr. Rick, please introduce me to my new friend."

I led Olga into the guest room. Ellen was lying in bed with her eyes wide open.

"Ellen, my good friend, I haven't seen you in a long time. Let's have some tea."

Olga told me that she was simply creating a new reality for Ellen, one that would seem familiar to her.

Olga and I led Ellen into the kitchen and sat her at the table while I prepared the tea. She sat next to Ellen and talked nonstop as if they were the best of friends.

"Olga, I have to go to my office. Here's my card. Call me on the cell phone if you have any questions at all."

"You leave everything to Olga, Mr. Rick. I will take good care of your Ellen."

My day at the office could have been 10 years long. I wasn't prepared for what I'd encounter that evening.

⚒

I never keep secrets from colleagues, especially my boss, Barbara Auletta. Bennie and I met with her and explained everything about Ellen. Barbara, who I always think of as a tough cookie, was in tears. She and Ellen had become close friends, and it was obvious that she was upset.

"Rick, you're the best agent I've got, and I want you to know that you have my 100 percent support. I'll help you get through this, but I'm not sure what I can do."

I went to my office and poured myself a cup of decaf—because Ellen had told me to knock off the caffeine. I'd never been so stressed in my life, but I decided to let Ellen's program take over. One of my jobs, like that of any FBI agent, is to think clearly under pressure. Bennie had once told me that you shouldn't try to force out negative thoughts. Rather, I should let the thoughts happen and observe them, just like in meditation. If you try to force them out, they will take control. So I let the horrible memories of the past two days sink in.

I got up from my desk and removed my jacket and shoes. I performed the five basic yoga exercises that Ellen taught me. Then I meditated for 20 minutes. For some strange reason—maybe not so strange—following Ellen's plan for stress management gave me comfort. My wife came up with a plan to aid my mental health, and now she doesn't even recognize me.

Okay, enough bullshit. I've got work to do, I thought. I've got a case to work on. I have to learn everything I can about surface-to-air missiles. But my thoughts were in one direction only. How can

I work a case when the love of my life is disappearing from me? Wait. What the hell am I thinking? Something's going on, and it's more than my personal crisis. There's an old saying that "shit happens." Well, sure it does, but usually in small increments. You get a flat tire or your washing machine craps out. Shit happens, but not large-scale shit like Dr. Harry talked about with the vast increase in dementia cases. Shit like that does not just happen. Shit like that happens for a reason. There's always a reason. There's always a pattern, and it usually begins with something that's not supposed to happen.

Something out of the blue, in and of itself, usually means there's a dot, a dot that wants to be connected to another dot. Dr. Harry told me about the dramatic and unforeseen increase in apparent dementia cases across the country, early-onset cases, *extremely* early-onset. And all the victims are women, young women. This has nothing to do with baby boomers. A huge number of the new cases involve the children of baby boomers, daughters of baby boomers, people in their 30s and 40s. Harry told me and Bennie about that guy Dr. Frank Buchannan, an epidemiologist, a medical detective. I hope Doctor Frank likes his new partner, Rick Bellamy, a guy he hasn't met.

Dr. Frank Buchannan may have some keys in his pocket that he doesn't know are there.

# CHAPTER NINETEEN

Marla Giovanni, Senior Vice President of Microsoft, met with her product development team, Jane Wilcox, Roger Boynton, and Phil Smith. The subject was the progress of one of Microsoft's biggest projects, the next version of Windows.

Phil Smith poured coffee for everyone as Giovanni took her seat at the head of the table.

"I'm going to go out on a hook, Marla," said assistant vice-president Jane Wilcox "and say that this will be the most exciting version of Windows that any of us ever imagined. It's almost making my head explode." Her other two colleagues nodded in agreement.

"Oh, my God," said Giovanni, "your head is going to explode?" The look of fear on Giovanni's face was clear.

"Well," said Wilcox, "you know me. I love to speak in superlatives when I'm excited about something. And this version of Windows definitely has me excited."

"But I like *these* windows," said Giovanni, pointing to the view through the real window in her office.

Everyone laughed, assuming that Giovanni was joking.

"Look at this," said Roger Boynton as he pressed his remote toward the viewing screen.

"I don't want to look at that, I want to look at *that*." Giovanni got up and walked over to the window and wiped off a smudge with a napkin. She then grabbed her chair, wheeled it away from the conference table, and placed it facing the window.

"Hey, Marla," said Wilcox, "I know how busy you are. Maybe you and I should huddle for a couple of minutes and get the rest of the gang back here tomorrow." Wilcox was trying to save a situation that was heading in a strange direction.

"Good idea," said both Boynton and Smith. They could see what Wilcox was trying to do. They walked out of the office, leaving Marla Giovanni and Jane Wilcox alone.

"Marla, what's up? We've been friends for years. Talk to me."

"Who are you?"

<hr />

An ambulance took Marla Giovanni to the nearby hospital at 4 p.m., where she was scheduled for a mental evaluation. Jane Wilcox went with her.

"Marla, honey, I don't know what the hell is going on but I'm with you."

"Who are you?"

# CHAPTER TWENTY

I arrived at the apartment early at 5:30 p.m. I couldn't wait to see Ellen. At the same time, I was scared shitless to see Ellen.

Olga met me at the door. Her smiling enthusiastic face was not there. Her Ukrainian accent had gotten thicker. She looked, well there's only one way to put it, she looked scared.

"Meester Reek, come seet and talk."

"Is everything okay, Olga?" Starting a conversation with a stupid question always does the trick.

"Ellen is not good. From this morning to now, she is getting worse. Every time I see her, she doesn't know me. I ask her questions, and she says nothing. She even..." Olga let go of a sob, blew her nose, and wiped the tears from her eyes. "Ellen has started peeing on herself. She doesn't even call me to go to the bathroom. She has no control. Also, she is very nervous."

"Did you call Doctor Bennie, Olga?"

"Yes, he comes here soon, maybe ten minutes."

The bell rang and Olga answered it. When Bennie walked in, she broke down in tears again.

"You can go, Olga," said Bennie. "Rick and I will take care of things."

"No, I stay. I sleep on couch. I will not leave Ellen."

Olga gave Bennie the rundown of the day as she had told me.

"Rick and I need to have a private chat, Olga."

"Okay, Doctor Bennie. I go into other room. I need for to take a nap."

———

Ben sat across from me at the kitchen table. He looked like a man about to say something that he'd rather not say.

"Rick, I cannot fucking believe what's happened in the past three days. But it did happen, and it is happening. Ellen needs round-the-clock nursing care, not just a visiting nurse like Olga, but a full-time staff with doctors on the standby. You can't turn this apartment into a full-care facility. It won't work."

"Bennie, are you telling me I have to put Ellen in an institution?"

"The word institution is loaded with negative implications, Rick. What I'm telling you is that Ellen needs to be moved to a nursing facility."

I lost it. I bawled my fucking brains out. In three days, Ellen went from a bright and beautiful woman to a person in need of full-time mental and physical care. But it was time to suck it up. Bennie was right.

"When Olga called me," Bennie said, "I put two and two together and made a few phone calls. There's a place just a few blocks from here called New Horizons. The director is a personal friend who owes me some favors. It's a good place, and I'll be on top of the situation."

Olga insisted on staying over. She slept on a cot in Ellen's room.

The next morning at 8 a.m., my Ellen was taken by ambulance to New Horizons.

Ellen Bellamy, age 38, best-selling author and Architect of the Year according to *Architectural Digest* magazine, now lives in a nursing home.

# CHAPTER TWENTY-ONE

"Bennie, it's Rick. I've arranged a meeting tomorrow at 10 at my office with Harry Noonan and that epidemiologist guy Buchannan. I'd like you to be there."

The next morning, we sat in the conference room across the hall from my office. My assistant brought in coffee and some bagels and rolls.

The day before, I had spent over an hour on the phone with Buchannan. He filled me in on his findings to date, and I told him everything about Ellen.

Frank Buchannan, age 47, was a slender, studious-looking guy, about 6'1" with reading glasses permanently ensconced on the end of his nose. He had close-cropped brown hair.

Bennie spoke before the meeting formally began.

"Rick, I visited Ellen this morning at New Horizons. It wasn't visiting time, but my friend put me down as one of her attending physicians. Hey, buddy, I can only imagine what you're going through. Your smart and beautiful wife is now under full-time care. It must suck."

"Bennie, thanks for your support as always, my friend. But I want to emphasize something to the three of you guys. I'm not sitting in front of you as Bennie's friend or as a man whose world just crumbled around him. Nope. I've called this meeting as an FBI agent. I'm a man trained to look at facts in a cold and hard way. And that's what this meeting is about. Doctor Harry blew our minds the other day when he talked about the sudden big uptick in new dementia cases, and especially the huge increase in early-onset victims. I've asked Frank Buchannan to join us because, as an epidemiologist or medical detective, he can help us take a cold, hard look at some weird shit."

"Rick, have you uncovered anything that I may have missed so far?" said Buchannan.

"No, I haven't, Frank, but let me take you on a brief tour through the brain of an FBI agent. Any time I see something big, something that shouldn't happen, a Black Swan, if you will, my antenna goes up. To turn the old phrase on its head, shit doesn't just happen, shit happens for a reason. The reason is usually the result of a bunch of connected dots that form a pattern. It's possible that this has nothing to do with law enforcement; in which case, I'm no longer needed. But remember Peter Falk, the rumpled detective in the old TV series, *Colombo*? Well, I'm like Colombo, 'Something's botherin me.' And until I rule out as many possible dots as I can, I suspect some bad shit is going on. I suspect it because that's what I've been trained to do. At this point, I have no idea what may be happening, but I've got to sort it out. Frank, I assume that you have every case entered into a database."

"That's right, Rick. We plug in a bunch of criteria, just like you, to see if there are any patterns."

"Please tell me about the criteria, Frank."

"Sure, it's fairly simple, Rick. We look at age, economic status, occupation, medical history, family history, and geographic location."

"And does your medical history include incidents of trauma, like accidents, assaults, or events like that?"

"Alzheimer's or any form of dementia, theoretically, can be caused by trauma, but it's rare, so we don't pay much attention to that."

Bennie jumped in and took the words out of my mouth.

"Hold the fucking phone," said Bennie, lapsing into his NYPD vocabulary. "First, Harry over here, the Alzheimer's maven, told us that you guys doubt that this disease is even Alzheimer's. Secondly, and I'm speaking as a doctor, how can you be so sure that trauma can't have something to do with this, especially since we're not sure what 'this' is?"

I wanted to keep Dr. Frank focused on the discussion, and I was concerned that Bennie's broadside may have gotten into his head and made him feel defensive.

"Hey, Frank, don't worry about it," I said. "When I investigate cases, I start with a lot of assumptions. But one thing I've learned over the years is that assumptions can kill a case. So the first thing I do when I start digging is to trash all of my assumptions, even if they seem well founded."

Buchannan didn't appear to be offended at all. He seemed like a guy who has his ego well under control. Thank God for that, I thought. The last thing I need on this team is bruised egos, looking to make excuses.

"You know," said Buchannan, "I have to admit something. I have a lot to learn from you law enforcement types, especially from Bennie, who's also a doctor. So, yes, we assumed that trauma has little or nothing to do with this condition, but that assumption was based on the prior theory that we were looking at Alzheimer's."

"If I may suggest something," said Dr. Harry, the Alzheimer's expert, "maybe we should stop calling this disease Alzheimer's, because we're not sure what the hell it is."

"Good point, Harry," said Bennie. "The one critical fact we have is the autopsies. I know from my general reading, and my conversations with you, that our way of diagnosing Alzheimer's has come a long way in the past few years. There was a time when we'd take a guess that a person had Alzheimer's, not just dementia. But the one slam-dunk piece of proof has always been the autopsy. That would rule the disease in or out. What we've learned, according to you guys, is that of the 10 people who died, not one of them actually had Alzheimer's. Not one. They had something that looked exactly like Alzheimer's from a diagnostic point of view, but the physical markers were just not there when the autopsy was performed. So, Doctor Frank, is it not a good idea to look at trauma, assuming that we may not be dealing with Alzheimer's?"

"You're right, Ben," said Frank, "you're dead-on right. I'm going to change our protocol right now, thanks to you law enforcement guys. I can even go backward. All I have to do is interview next of kin to ask about incidents of trauma and then plug that information into the database. Hell, it wasn't until the late 19th Century when Louis Pasteur nailed down germ theory once and for all. Before him, the medical community thought that infection was caused by miasma or fetid water vapor. Thank you guys for reminding me that we haven't gotten to the end of medical science."

"How soon can you plug in the data on trauma, Frank?" asked Bennie.

"No problem, Ben. Since these early-onset numbers started coming in, grant and government money flowed behind it. I can hire a small army of researchers, which is exactly what I'm going to do."

"Okay, guys," I said, "let's see where we are and where we're going from here. First, we've concluded that we're probably not dealing with Alzheimer's, but a disease that mimics its symptoms. Let's call it *The Syndrome*. Next, we don't have reliable data on trauma, which the good Doctor Frank will supply us. Next, I'm going to need Frank's entire database to turn over to FBI researchers. You can't connect dots unless you see the dots."

"Rick, I'm sure you understand that I'll need a court order to release that data. I'm sure you can get it with a phone call."

"No problem, Frank. I do things by the book. Barbara Auletta knows we're meeting today and what the subject of the meeting is. She's already cleared it with Sarah Watson, Director of the FBI."

"Rick, Ben, if you don't mind me asking a question," said Buchannan, "and maybe it's a naive question, but why are you guys so focused on evidence of trauma?"

"Because bad guys can cause trauma."

# CHAPTER TWENTY-TWO

S ister Doris Augusta had just taken over as principal of
St. Mary's Elementary School in the Ridgewood, Queens
section of New York City. Because of severe budget cuts, the
Archdiocese of Brooklyn, which controlled all Catholic schools
in the area, had consolidated three elementary schools into
one, St. Mary's. The building was designed to accommodate
300 kids, but the enrollment was suddenly 395. Three mobile
trailers had been brought to the property to accommodate the
new children.

"Sister, it looks like we have a bad water leak in the main building," said Kirsi Almati, her assistant.

Great way to start a new job, thought Sister Augusta.

"Did you call a plumber?"

"Yes, sister, I called Sparkle Plumbing on Metropolitan Avenue.
I hear that they're good and fast."

Muhamad Islam, walked into the main office of Sparkle Plumbing. He had been hired four weeks before as an assistant. Joe Raboni, the manager, sat behind his desk.

"Muhamad, we just got a call from St. Mary's School around the corner. Bad leak in the main building. Get there as soon as you can. Bring Jack O'Leary with you. Here are the keys to the truck."

In the back of the truck were various supplies and plumbing tools. Stacked up next to the cab were four 40-pound boxes of Tannerite. All of the containers had been mixed.

At 11:30 a.m., all of the children at St. Mary's were in the large schoolyard enjoying recess before lunch. I can't believe our little school now has 395 kids, thought Sister Augusta.

The Sparkle Plumbing truck entered the property, with a teacher's aide clearing a way through the crowds of children.

Muhamad Islam pressed the detonator of his device as the truck came to a stop next to the building, while yelling "Allahu Akbar" three times.

The blast crumbled the aging school, with its three floors cascading down to the earth. The explosion also stormed out in all directions, killing 125 children and injuring dozens more. The three mobile trailers were flung like shoeboxes, one landing in the middle of the road in front of the school. Sister Augusta's body was found the next day under one of the mobile trailers.

The sound of ambulances and police cars jarred the afternoon in the quiet neighborhood, as the area hospitals filled up quickly with the broken little bodies of the children who survived.

⭤

My job involves a lot of unpleasant shit, but the St. Mary's School bombing was the most sickening disaster I'd ever seen. It wasn't just a crime scene. It was a place of monstrous depravity, a killing field of innocent children. I had been tipped by our friend

Imam Mike from Brooklyn that something may have been afoot at a school. Mike is our most trusted mole, a man who has his eyes and ears to the sights and sounds of radical Islam. But all Mike was able to tell me was that some radicals were upset about the crowding of children, and a mixing of sexes, in schools. Obviously, it wasn't a tip that I was able to act on, because crowded schools exist all over the country.

We suspected terrorism immediately, and I was put in charge of the crime scene. Fifteen other agents were with me, and the local NYPD police captain provided me with plenty of cops to help.

Cops and FBI agents are usually a tough crowd. Law enforcement brings you into contact with a lot of mayhem, ugly mayhem. But these officers were having a hard time dealing with the disgusting scene before them, and so was I. There is something about seeing a cop in tears that jolts your emotions. It got worse as parents started to show up. The forensic people were doing their best to identify the little bodies, but a lot of those little bodies had been blown to bits. Because I had been researching the use of Tannerite in terrorist bombings, I made sure that the CSI people focused on bomb residue.

I left the scene at 6 p.m. that evening. John Scarpetta, one of my colleagues at the bureau, took over for me.

The St. Mary's attack would focus the efforts of the FBI as well as the NYPD for months to come. Because I was up to my ears in *The Syndrome* investigation, not to mention the surface-to-air missile operation, Barbara Auletta relieved me of any involvement in the St. Mary's atrocity. I felt relieved, not just to have my caseload lightened, but because it sickened me to investigate the murder of little children.

I got back to my apartment at 7 p.m., my empty apartment. Whenever I had a particularly rough day, I could always count on Ellen to focus me, to calm me down; but, of course, Ellen wasn't there. She was at New Horizons Nursing Home.

# CHAPTER TWENTY-THREE

B efore I turned on the TV this morning to catch up on the news, I read my index card for a Jerry Seinfeld joke. I needed a laugh after yesterday's horror at St. Mary's School. But I couldn't laugh. Otherwise, Ellen's prescription for my de-stressing was working. Ellen, a woman who doesn't know who she is or who I am. I planned to see her at New Horizons before I went to the office.

Shepard Smith appeared on the TV.

"I have terrible news to bring you this morning, folks. Our Fox News producers have just told me that there has been yet another surface-to-air missile attack on an American aircraft. United flight 301 had just taken off from Dallas/Fort Worth International Airport when it was struck by what appears to be a surface-to-air missile, a SAM. There are also reports that a drone aircraft was seen in the vicinity of the missile launch. We have an unconfirmed report that the drone fired its own missile toward the launch area, but the weapon was either a dud or it simply missed. The grim reality, and I say this with all sympathy for the loved ones of the passengers, is that the plane crashed in a ball of fire, and authorities don't believe that there are any survivors of the 259 passengers and crew. We'll be keeping our viewers up to date on this breaking story as more facts come in."

I knew I should get to the office, as people would be going crazy over the latest plane attack, but no way in hell was I going to skip seeing Ellen.

⊨⊨ ⊨⊨

"Any changes, Nancy?" I asked Ellen's nurse.

"The good news, Rick, is that she's stable. She has moments of lucidity, such as this morning when I brought her breakfast. She was delighted that scrambled eggs were on the menu."

"Ellen hates scrambled eggs."

Nancy, who could give seminars on bedside manner, patted me on the arm.

"Rick, it's one day at a time. Let's thank God for small favors. Hey, she now enjoys something she never liked before."

Ellen was dozing. I leaned over her bed and kissed her on the forehead. Her skin still had that same wonderful aroma. I wiped a tear from my eye.

"My allergies are acting up," Mr. Tough Guy lied to Nurse Nancy.

⊨⊨ ⊨⊨

I hadn't been in my office for more than five minutes when Buster walked in.

"What the hell is the story with that drone in Dallas?" I said.

"The news got it right. The drone's missile was a fucking dud. With these missile patrols that we've launched, you only get one shot to make it right. One dud and 259 bodies. The only good news is that they caught the missile shooter. He's in a lockup right now, but he asked to make the phone call. So Mr. Servant of Allah is now lawyered up and not talking. I wish they'd let me interrogate the scumbag."

"Hey, Buster, don't forget your yoga, meditation, and joke reading. Ellen gave us all a regime to follow in our crazy business."

"Tell me about Ellen, Rick. How's it going?"

"Nothing new, Buster. I guess the only good thing to report is that she now likes scrambled eggs. But she doesn't recognize me, and that tears me apart."

I then brought Buster up to speed on my meeting with Drs. Buchannan, Noonan, and Bennie.

"The statistics are too crazy to be an accident, Buster. Until I can rule out any possible intentional acts, I'm going to pursue it."

"Bennie tells me that the epidemiologist is giving you all of the names of the victims of *The Syndrome*, as you've named it. I suggest we plug the names into our database at the agency. My guys know how to play around with algorithms better than those medical types."

"I'll have it to you in the morning."

"Rick, talk to me. Do you really think there may be some connection between *The Syndrome* and everything else that's going on?"

"Buster, I don't know. Bennie told me that he thinks I'm indulging in a fantasy to try to make sense of what happened to Ellen. But I told Ben, and I'm telling you, I'm doing this as an FBI agent. If I don't find anything, so be it. But if I don't look, I'm guaranteed not to find anything."

"Rick, I think of myself as a tough guy, a hardnosed spook, but what you're going through with that wonderful wife of yours has me sick. I'm glad you're throwing yourself into your work. It's all you can do. And knowing you, if there's something to be found, you'll find it."

Comforting words from my friend, but he didn't know as he spoke that I was about to learn of some dots, some large dots.

# CHAPTER TWENTY-FOUR

The next morning, I was in my office when the phone rang. It was Dr. Frank Buchannan. He asked to meet with me.

"Buster, it's Rick. I just got a call from Doctor Buchannan. He's peeing in his pants to see me. I think you should be in this meeting too. He'll be here in a few minutes, and Bennie is on his way."

Frank Buchannan was in my office in 20 minutes.

"What's up, Frank?" I said, after introducing him to Buster.

"Well, Rick, as I said last time, you FBI guys are teaching me a thing or two. What I'm about to show you will mess with your fucking minds." Tough words from my mild-mannered intellectual friend. This guy's on to something, I thought.

"I have a list of victims of *The Syndrome* just from the past month. It represents 10 percent of all new cases."

"Take it from the top, Frank. Please give us your summary first and then drill down into the particulars."

"Okay, here it is. All are women. All are young. The oldest is 42. And here's an interesting piece of data: all of them can be characterized as 'prominent.' My researchers tag a result as prominent when the woman has an important title or position. Your wife, of course, partner at a major architectural firm, is on the list. These are just a few of the names that just showed up in the past five days.

"Georgina Laughlin, age 42, Secretary of Commerce;

"Mary Escobedo, age 36, CEO of Suresoft, a large technical conglomerate;

"Jane Lopez, age 40, Secretary of the Interior;

"Florence Lambda, age 37, Deputy Secretary of Defense;

"Dolores Estrada, age 41, Senior Director, NASA;

"Aimee Pierce, age 34, CEO of United Way. Ms. Pierce just showed up on our database yesterday."

Buchannan's cell phone went off.

"I'm sorry, but I had to leave this thing on because I'm expecting some stuff that may be important for this meeting.

"Just email what you're telling me," Buchannan said to his assistant.

In a couple of minutes, Frank checked his email and read us the results.

"Oh my God! These just came in this morning, between the time I left Columbia Presbyterian and when I arrived here.

"Rebecca Spellman, age 38, Deputy Secretary of the Treasury;

"Alberta Newman, age 39, President of Oberlin College;

"Juanita Mazur, age 40, newly elected congresswoman from Georgia;

"Marilyn Stockman, age 36, CEO of Advank Publishing Company;

"Nancy McLaughlin, age 40, Deputy Secretary of Agriculture;

"Marla Giovanni, age 39, Senior Vice President, Microsoft;

"Wanda Black—and get this poor woman's age—25, Deputy Secretary of Labor."

"Dear God," Bennie said.

"Gentlemen, somebody is targeting young prominent women," Frank said. "And I remind you, the list I just read is from the last two hours."

"Targeting?" Buster said. "How the hell do you target an unsuspecting person with *The Syndrome*? We don't even know what it is."

"Frank," Bennie said, "have you adjusted at all for gender and age over the same time period as you've discussed?"

"Yes. The results aren't included in the list I just gave you, but the numbers are shocking. Of the few hundred people who have come down with Alzheimer's type symptoms in the past month, the only ones who are under the age of 50 are all women. Of the men, the average age is in the 70s, which is what we would expect from Alzheimer's. *The Syndrome* is something new on the radar."

"Unless we can throw statistics and logic out the window," I said, "we're looking at an inescapable conclusion. An intelligent actor or actors are involved. This shit is happening on purpose."

Frank Buchannan's phone went off. He looked at his email. Then looked up at us.

"In the past 20 minutes, there have been 53 more cases of young prominent women with *The Syndrome*."

Buster grabbed his phone and went to a corner of the room.

"Who are you calling?" I asked.

"CIA Director Carlini. We need to take this to the White House."

# CHAPTER TWENTY-FIVE

I walked into the Waldorf Astoria, along with Barbara Auletta, Ben, and Buster for a must-attend dinner. The purpose of the event was to honor people in law enforcement. About 1,500 other FBI and CIA agents were there, along with other law enforcement officers from around the country. The keynote speaker was Amanda Reynolds, First Lady of the United States. Amanda Reynolds is one of the most popular First Ladies ever. As is tradition, First Ladies always take on an issue they can call their own. Often it's child protection, literacy, or health, anything that doesn't conflict head-on with something on the table at the White House.

Amanda Reynolds, age 41, was an FBI agent for the five years immediately after she graduated from Harvard Law School. When her husband took office as president, she assumed a different role from the one First Ladies usually adopt. Her passion was raising esteem for law enforcement people. Tall, at 5'10", pretty, with long brown hair, and a commanding voice, Amanda was a hit. Her approval polls always put her in the upper 90s. She also had a reputation as one of the best public speakers in the country, man or woman. She was also one of my favorite people, although I never met her personally.

Senator Hugh Jackson was the Chairman of the Homeland Security Committee. A close ally of President Reynolds, Jackson was also a family friend, and he was the emcee for the dinner.

"Ladies and gentlemen," said Jackson, "it almost sounds like a cliché to say that we have a special treat for you this evening, but it's true—we do have a treat. Our keynote speaker is none other than Amanda Reynolds, First Lady of the United States. She's also one of the best friends the law enforcement community ever had. After she graduated from Harvard Law School, Amanda didn't follow her classmates to Wall Street. No, she chose public service, and spent the first five years of her career as an FBI agent, rising to the position of Deputy Director. Amanda knows a thing or two about law enforcement.

"I won't delay any further. Ladies and gentlemen, it is my pleasure and honor to introduce the First Lady of the United States, a woman most of us know as America's Girlfriend."

The audience stood, applauded, and cheered for what seemed like five minutes. Amanda walked to the podium. Hugh Jackson leaned over to kiss her on the cheek. What did I just see? Amanda seemed to pull away, as if she were repulsed by Jackson's polite show of friendship. I wasn't the only one who saw this. A guy seated near me said, "What the hell was *that* all about?" I also heard a few say, "What the fuck?"

Amanda stood before the microphone. The cheering had died down, and the room was silent, anticipating a talk from a great orator.

A minute went by, then two. I'm a pretty good judge of people, and I got a sense—a sense that I tried to dismiss—that Amanda Reynolds was confused. She finally spoke.

"Thank you, Jimmy."

Jimmy? Did Hugh Jackson have a new nickname?

She continued to stare out into the large audience. Then she spoke again.

"The chicken sucked," she said, apparently referring to one of the dinner selections. Amanda Reynolds is known for her sense of humor, but it usually doesn't accompany earthy language.

The crowd chuckled politely.

A guy called out, "Why don't you tell us about your FBI career." That was totally uncalled for, but most of us in the audience were happy that he had broken the awkward pressure.

"What's an FBI?"

The audience was silent. The tension in the room was getting painful.

"What's this all about?"

The audience laughed, all of us thinking, hoping, that this was a joke. I looked at Bennie, who sat next to me. He closed his eyes and put his hand to his forehead.

"Who are you people?"

I thought this was just a lead up to something like "You people are the backbone of our public safety," or some positive sentiment like that.

She took a sip of water and went into a coughing fit. After she stopped coughing, she turned to Hugh Jackson, who was seated behind her on the dais.

"Jimmy, why are all these people looking at me? What the fuck is going on?"

I didn't think in words. My mind carried me back to a horrible memory, when I came home and realized that my Ellen was beginning to lose her mind. I had that same sickening feeling as I watched Amanda Reynolds.

Jackson, a skilled politician known for his statesmanlike ability to make the best of tense situations, stood and approached the podium. Without turning off the microphone, he said, loud enough for everyone to hear, "Amanda, why don't you sit down and relax? I'll handle it from here."

He then turned to the audience and said, "We're going to take a short break, folks."

Jackson was trying his best to unscramble the eggs.

The following day, Amanda Reynolds was admitted to Walter Reed Medical Facility for psychiatric evaluation. The preliminary diagnosis was sudden-onset dementia, with all the symptoms of Alzheimer's disease. She was 41 years old.

# CHAPTER TWENTY-SIX

Barbara Auletta, Buster, Bennie, and I, along with CIA Director Carlini, waited in the Oval Office for our meeting with the president. Dr. Frank Buchannan and Dr. Harry Noonan were there also. We had expected that President Reynolds would skip the meeting under the circumstances. Reynolds strode into the room and walked to the front of his desk. He's is a big man, about 6'3", with broad shoulders. The President is a commanding figure. We prepared for a stirring speech, a sad, inspiring speech, but he began in a way I didn't expect.

"Who's Rick Bellamy?"

I raised my hand. He strode over to me and I stood, of course. I offered my hand, but instead he wrapped me in a bear hug. He grabbed me by the shoulders and looked me in the eyes, tears streaming down his face.

"Rick, you and I are members of a brotherhood, a strange fucking brotherhood."

It was obvious that the poor man was distraught over what he learned last night. If he was looking for sympathy, he turned to the right guy.

Reynolds walked to his place in front of his desk. He straightened his shoulders, obviously trying his best to compose himself.

"Ladies and gentlemen, this isn't a press conference so I'm going to cut the bullshit. A few months ago, you heard me announce that World War III had begun. Nothing has happened between then and now to make me change my mind. We're at war. Last night I found out that the woman I love, Amanda, the First Lady, has come down with this goddamned illness that we've been reading about. You don't need to be a CIA or an FBI agent to see the outline of what's going on. On my way here, Doctor Buchannan briefed me on what he'll tell us this morning. Any update, Frank? Just the numbers, please."

"Mr. President, since yesterday, the list of young prominent American women who have been stricken has grown to 850."

We all gasped.

"My friends, as I said, you don't need to be a secret agent to see what's happening," said the president. "We see what's going on, but we don't know what it is. I'm not going to give you any politically correct bullshit. These cases are intentional. Because of its cruelty and depravity, I'm making a preliminary guess that it's al-Qaeda or ISIS, or some other inhuman bastards associated with them. But, to beat the obvious over the head with a stick, we have no idea how they're doing it."

⚔

Gloria Franken, the President's secretary, appeared in the doorway. Reynolds looked at her with raised eyebrows. Obviously, her appearance was totally against protocol.

"I'm sorry, sir, but a gentlemen called and said that he has to speak to Agent Bellamy immediately. I explained that he was in a high-level meeting with you, sir, but he said that his message has a direct impact on the meeting."

"Grab the call, Rick. I hope your friend isn't inviting you to a bowling game."

Reynolds' little joke helped ease the stress of the meeting. I went to the outer office to take the call.

"Rick, it's Mike, Imam Mike from Brooklyn."

Mike, aka Muhammed Busharif, is the imam of a mosque in Brooklyn. He's a trusted inside source, one of the few we've got. He gradually became infuriated with all of the terrorist killings in the name of his religion. When a good friend of his daughter was killed in a bomb attack at a football game, Mike went over the edge. He's renounced his religion, but only to Buster, me, and Bennie. Mike's language tends to be salty, not what you'd expect from a religious leader. Mike's on our side, and is probably the most important mole we've ever had. Mike feeds us information that we could never get without an insider like him. He's also a good guy. He was one of the first to offer me his condolences when he heard about Ellen.

"Mike, what's up? You know I'm at the White House meeting with the president."

"Rick, I know you're talking about some heavy shit, but I'm about to tell you some *really* heavy shit."

"Mike, how can I express that you have my undivided attention? So what is it?"

"I've been hearing constant chatter about water bottles. Yes, water bottles. But then I started to hear about water bottles in the same sentence as 'heathen bitches.' This morning, I overheard a reference to Ellen Bellamy, your lovely wife."

"Mike, did you hear anything specific about these bottles, anything that could be a link to something more?"

"I don't have a clue, Rick, not a fucking clue. I've been reading in the papers about young women coming down with a horrible disease, just like Ellen. When I started to hear about 'heathen bitches' and water bottles in the same sentence, I knew I had to call you."

"God bless you, Mike. Please keep your ear to the ground and let me know when you hear anything else. Oh, and Mike, watch your ass. Be safe my friend."

I walked back into the Oval Office. President Reynolds gestured for me to speak.

I was about to simply relate what Imam Mike had told me when I just blurted out, "Holy shit!"

"Could you be a bit more specific, Rick?" said Reynolds.

I felt like I was going to faint. I just connected a dot in my head, a dot to my conversation with Imam Mike. I sat down and wiped the sweat off my forehead.

"I just found out what happened to Ellen. I just found out what probably happened to the First Lady and all the other women. They were sprayed with what looks like water bottles. After I got off the phone with my contact, I remembered something that Ellen told me. She said that some jerk who was washing the windows on our building sprayed her in the face with a water bottle. He said, 'Happy springtime.' She was angry but let it go, thinking that the guy was just flirting. I put in a call to building management, but was told that the guy had left."

"Dear God," said President Reynolds. "We hosted a bunch of kids on the great lawn a couple of days ago. Part of their game was to squirt water bottles at each other. Amanda was sprayed in the face by an adult, who immediately apologized. The Secret Service wanted to talk to the guy, but he was gone in an instant.

"Rick, who was that call from and what did you just find out?" said Reynolds.

"The caller was Muhammed Busharif, an imam of a mosque in Brooklyn, Mr. President. He's a turncoat, the best kind. He's turned to our side and is probably our best inside source about radical Islamic activities. Bennie and Buster know him well. He finally renounced his religion when a good friend of his daughter was killed at the Notre Dame football bombing last year. He just told me that he's been hearing a lot of chatter about water bottles in the same sentence as the phrase 'heathen bitches.' That's what my outburst was about when I came back to the room. I remembered Ellen being sprayed in the face by a water bottle."

"I'd like some medical input here," said Reynolds. "Is it possible that it's a poison, a virus, or a bacteria that can cause a disease that looks like Alzheimer's? Doctor Frank?"

"The answer is that I simply don't know, but I think the evidence we just heard points to something in water bottles that could be causing these incidents. I need to study this, fast."

"And me as well," said Dr. Harry Noonan, the Alzheimer's expert.

"Let's hear your thoughts, people," said Reynolds. "This is now a working meeting, and I'm part of the team."

"Buster?" said Director Carlini. "I can hear your brain clicking from here. What do you think?"

"Here's where we are, at least from a working hypothesis point of view. The young women who have come down with *The Syndrome* were sprayed in the face by a water bottle, which contained a substance we know nothing about. But why women, and why women who we've been calling prominent?"

"Could it be that they're being punished for some perceived slight to Islam?" I said. "When Ellen was kidnapped last year, she emptied an AK-47 into an al-Qaeda big shot. That would make her a clear target for revenge."

"The First Lady," said Reynolds, "has been quite public with her denunciation of the way radical Islamists treat women."

"If we drill down into the list of the targeted women," said Buster, "I'm sure we're going to find reasons why they were singled out by radicals."

"But here's the most important thing," said the president, "we have to lay our hands on one of those bottles, and then we have to study what's in it and see if we can come up with something to prevent it."

"Or cure it, Mr. President?" I added.

"Your lips to God's ears, Rick.

"Folks," the President continued. "This operation, if we can call it an operation, is the most crucial item on the nation's agenda. Someone or some group is attacking young prominent women. We've got to stop it."

# CHAPTER TWENTY-SEVEN

"This is Wolf Blitzer reporting for CNN. We received a shocking announcement this morning from the White House. First Lady Amanda Reynolds, age 41, has come down with the bizarre disease that is afflicting young women all across the country. She was about to address a law enforcement dinner at the Waldorf Astoria. According to eyewitnesses, the First Lady appeared to be confused and couldn't seem to find her words.

"The disease, which is being referred to as *The Syndrome*, mimics the symptoms of Alzheimer's disease. There are differences, however. A large majority of the women afflicted are quite young, much younger than people we'd expect to be hit with Alzheimer's. The average age over the past month of hundreds of cases reported is 39. The disease also appears to be tragically fast-acting. We've received many reports of a woman first showing symptoms one day, and in the advanced stages of dementia within 48 hours. Oddly, none of the victims are men, at least not in the early age group. Incidents of male Alzheimer's are what we would expect, with elderly people as the primary victims. Another odd twist to this story is the occupational profiles of the women. To put it simply, the victims appear to be among the most prominent women in the country, Amanda Reynolds being the most stunning example. Secretaries and deputy secretaries of large government agencies, as well as the female heads of major corporations, have fallen victim in the past few months.

"We've tried to get word from the White House, but have been told that the President will address the issue tomorrow. He is understandably distraught over the sudden illness of his wife, our First Lady. CNN will bring you updates on this troubling situation as they come in."

# CHAPTER TWENTY-EIGHT

"Peace be with you, Brother Musif. May Allah heap blessings upon you for the way you are handling the project we call The Scent of Revenge. The list of the heathen women we've attacked is growing. Tell me how everything is progressing with our factory in Baltimore."

"Brother Ali, the Baltimore plant is now fully operational. As you know, we are only able to produce small amounts of the substance each day, but our output is improving."

"And what about safety precautions? Did I not hear about a young brother who inhaled the substance recently and came down with the disease?"

"Yes, Ali, it happened. I have issued strict orders about how to handle the substance and what must be done to ensure the safety of our workers."

"How soon do you see us graduating from water bottles to larger delivery mechanisms?"

"At the rate our Baltimore plant is improving, Musif, I expect to see a larger device for delivering the substance. It will not be as direct as spray from a bottle, but soon we can debilitate thousands of infidels in a matter of minutes."

"Ali, perhaps it is not my place to ask, but why are we limiting our targets to women?"

"Musif, we are attacking the heathen breeders. Soon we will target younger women. After that, as our manufacturing capacity increases, we will deliver The Scent of Revenge to men as well. But for now, our plans are working perfectly."

"I must agree, Ali. Amanda Reynolds was our best target to date."

"Soon, Musif, the infidels will spend all of their money on hospitals and nursing homes."

# CHAPTER TWENTY-NINE

Ashley Patterson, age 38, was recently promoted to the rank of rear admiral in the United States Navy, making her the youngest admiral in the nation's history. A tall, beautiful African-American woman, Ashley is the subject of countless newspaper articles and TV appearances. She's the Navy's rising star. Her husband, Jack Thurber, is a Pulitzer Prize winning journalist.

When she was captain of the *USS Abraham Lincoln*, Ashley ordered an air attack on an Iranian *Alvand* Class frigate that had fired missiles at the *Lincoln*. As a result of the attack, the Iranian ship sank. Ashley Patterson is known as a tough and decisive military leader.

In April, Admiral Patterson commanded Carrier Strike Group 1115. Her flagship was the *USS Abraham Lincoln,* her old command. A strike group, which used to be called a battle group, consists of an aircraft carrier, the *Lincoln* in this case, a guided missile cruiser, and two frigates or large destroyers.

On April 16, Admiral Patterson walked along the flight deck with her aide, Captain Randolph Simmons, to inspect a plane that had a landing gear problem. A sailor, who was cleaning the air-craft, pointed a water bottle at the admiral, spraying her in the face.

"You're on report, sailor," Captain Simmons shouted. But the man was gone in an instant.

Two days later, at 8 a.m. on the morning of April 18, Carrier Strike Group 1115 prepared to get underway and head to sea from its homeport in Norfolk, Virginia. Admiral Patterson was ashore at a pre-deployment meeting. She walked up the gangplank as the shrill sound of the bosun's pipe sounded and the officer of the deck announced, "Carrier Strike Group 1115 arriving." This was the traditional Navy way of announcing an arriving dignitary along with his or her position or command. Captain Randolph Simmons, her aide, followed her. He noticed that the admiral failed to salute the American flag when she got to the top of the gangplank, and didn't return the salute of the officer of the deck, two serious breaches of military protocol.

The plan, as orchestrated by Simmons, called for Admiral Patterson to address the ship over the public address system from the quarterdeck, the area on a ship that served as the place of acting command when a ship was in port. Her words would be carried to the other ships in the Strike Group. He took the microphone from its holder and handed it to her.

"What's this for?" Admiral Patterson said, looking at Simmons.

"Would you rather address the Group from your office, Admiral?"

"I have an office?"

Captain Simmons, a 25-year veteran, had seen his share of difficult circumstances, including combat operations in the Gulf. But nothing prepared him for this. The admiral did seem a bit off that morning, he had noticed, but this behavior had him stumped. It is standard procedure for the commander of a Strike Group to address all of the ships' personnel before heading out to sea. Simmons figured he'd take the situation moment-to-moment.

"Yes, ma'am. Would you like me to show you to your office?"

"Do I know you? Why are you wearing that silly uniform? Who the hell are you anyway?"

"Get the admiral a cup of coffee, sailor," Simmons said to the quartermaster of the watch.

He led Ashley to a chair and suggested she have a seat. He stepped into a passageway next to the quarterdeck, picked up a phone off the bulkhead, and called the bridge.

"Bill, it's Randy Simmons," he said to the captain of the *Lincoln*. "Please come to the quarterdeck immediately. We have a situation here. I think you'll want to address the Strike Group yourself."

The deployment of Carrier Strike Group 1115 was delayed on orders of the Chief of Naval Operations.

Admiral Ashley Patterson, age 38, was taken by ambulance to the nearby naval hospital. After a short battery of tests, she was admitted with a diagnosis of severe dementia.

# CHAPTER THIRTY

Ellen sat in the dayroom by the window at the New Horizons Nursing Home. From there, she had a pleasant view of a landscaped courtyard. She wore a dark brown skirt that I had given her last Christmas, a pink blouse, a light blue cardigan sweater, and nursing-home-issued slippers. Her beautiful blond hair was cut short, something I had agreed to a few days ago. The nurse explained that it was better kept short for hygiene.

I sat in the chair next to her and opened a box of Perugina chocolates, her favorite. When I offered the box to her, she shook her head.

"How about a big smile, honey?"

"My name is Ellen."

"Okay, Ellen, how about a smile for your boyfriend?"

She continued to stare out the window, not looking at me. I stroked her hand as I looked at her. "Is that necessary?" she said as she pulled her hand away.

"No problem, honey, let's just sit and be with each other."

"My name is Ellen."

After a few minutes, Ellen looked at me with her wonderful smile. The little scar on her cheek turned into a dimple. She reached over and squeezed my hand.

"Daddy, where did you go?"

Bennie had been coaching me on how to act when I'm with Ellen. "Don't mess with her world, Rick," Bennie said. "Let yourself into it." Easy to say, but not easy to do when your wife thinks you're her father.

"I just had to go to the store, Ellen. Here, I brought you your favorite chocolates." I offered her the box again, but she wasn't interested.

I felt a tear run down my face. As I wiped it away, Ellen reached over and put her hand on my face and said, "It's okay, Daddy. Here, have a chocolate." Not wanting to disappoint her, I did, although I'm not crazy about chocolate.

After an hour, I stood, leaned over, and kissed her on the cheek. She didn't pull away. She didn't reciprocate, but she didn't pull away. I took that as progress.

As I walked through the lobby on my way to the door, I heard a voice.

"Hey, Rick, how about a cup of coffee?"

It was Nancy Langdon, one of Ellen's nurses. I had to get to the office, but I wanted to spend some time with Nancy so she could fill me in on Ellen's condition.

Nancy was a big woman, not fat, just big. She had a ruddy complexion and a pretty face.

"Nancy," I said as we sat down, "you know what I do for a living. I'm in a tough profession. One crisis after another winds up on my desk, but what happened to Ellen is the worst thing that ever happened in my life. I'll be honest with you; I'm having a tough time dealing with this. Ellen and I had a relationship that's hard to describe. I guess it's called love. Until a few days ago, she was vibrant, beautiful, and kind. I feel like I'm lost."

"Rick, I'm not going to coddle you. You're too big a boy for that. But I will tell you that we all appreciate what you're going through. I've dealt with dementia patients and their families for over 20 years. But there's a big difference between all of those cases and Ellen. The youngest Alzheimer's victim I ever cared for was 57 years old. The disease crept up slowly, as is the case most of the time. A family member gradually realizes that a loved one is slipping away. When we were told that this happened to Ellen within two days, we were in shock. You had no time to adjust, no time to slowly change things. Wham, you were hit in the face with a new reality. You and Ellen have been dealt a shitty hand, Rick. Here's my contact information. Call me at any time whenever you need to talk."

I didn't tell Nancy that the cards Ellen and I held were dealt by another human being, not fate. It's my job to hunt down the dealers.

I didn't like to think that I would hunt them down and kill them, but that's exactly what I planned to do.

# CHAPTER THIRTY-ONE

I'd just finished my cup of decaf in my office. I'm following Ellen's plan for fighting stress to the finest detail. Decaf coffee, yoga, meditation, thinking of a joke before answering the phone. Everything except for item number one—sex with Ellen. She also insisted that I shouldn't dwell on problems, just let them in and confront them. But it's time to stop stroking myself. It's time to get to work and find the scumbags who did this.

Bennie and Buster walked into my office for our planned meeting at 11 a.m.

"Did you hear about Admiral Patterson?" said Buster.

"Yes," I said, "I read about it in an email update from Frank Buchannan. Did you know her?"

"Yes, she and her husband, Jack, are good friends with both me and Bennie. First Ellen, and now Ashley Patterson. This shit is getting up-close and personal."

"Buster, we have to work fast, which I know is your favorite speed. So, what do you have for us?"

"We know what we're missing, guys, and President Reynolds knows it too," said Buster. "We know that *The Syndrome* is caused by a deliberate act, and we know it's done with spray bottles. What we don't know is the identity of the substance. Doctor Buchannan insists that if we discover the substance, we can come up with a vaccine. But until we find it, our heads are up our collective asses. Would you guys agree that our focus has to be to discover the substance?"

"Buster, as usual, you've hit it on the head. So now I'm going to raise the obvious question. How the hell do we find the stuff?"

"Imam Mike," Bennie said. "That man is becoming the key player in this game. He told Rick about the water bottles and the comments about 'infidel bitches.' What are the odds that Mike can lay his hands on a bottle of the shit?"

"Hey, we have to be careful with our friendly imam," said Buster. "The last thing we want is for him to get whacked. He's a great guy and a team player, but I'm worried that he's getting a bit too excited with his role as a born-again spy. I don't think we should encourage Mike to take a proactive role. Let him just listen and report what he hears. And he *is* plugged into the radical fringes of Islam. It's just a matter of time before he comes up with a lead, just like he came up with the clue about the water bottles."

"I'm sure we've gone over this with our doctor friends," I said, "but am I correct that the few autopsies that have been performed found no evidence of any strange chemical or substance?"

"That's right," said Bennie. "No traces of any substances other than prescription drugs on any of the bodies. I spoke to Buchannan this morning. He has a hunch, an educated hunch, that we may be looking at a bacteria. It doesn't linger in the body for long. That could explain why the autopsies showed nothing."

"Hey, guys, look out the window," I said. "See that hotel over there. As we've been speaking, cleaning people have been spraying hundreds of squirts from bottles. See those window washers? Spray bottles are like another appendage for those guys. The bastard that sprayed Ellen was a window washer." I reached down into the bottom drawer of my desk. "Look at this—a spray bottle. I'm all in favor of basic police work, but how the hell can we focus on something that's all over the place?"

"Now that you mention it, Rick," said Buster, "any leads on the man who sprayed Ellen?"

"A dead end. We interviewed the other window washers who were on duty that day. They all said the guy just showed up as a temp employee. They never thought to ask questions, because that's the way things are done in that business. And keep in mind, the man who sprayed the First Lady was just an adult at a kid's game, not a cleaning person."

"Anything new on the profiles of the victims?" said Bennie.

"I think so. Joe Flynn, my database expert, is excited that he's on to something. He wanted some more time to finish his preliminary report. He'll be here after we break for lunch."

—⟨+⟩—

Joe Flynn came into our meeting at 1:30. Joe is a good man, a skilled researcher and a dogged fact checker. He's a great guy to have on your team; but he's a total computer geek, and sometimes it's difficult to get him to speak English.

"Joe, you've met Bennie and Buster. So tell us, what have you found so far on the victim profiles?"

"Well," Joe said as he adjusted his glasses, "first let me tell you how I developed the algorithm."

"Joe, my friend, fuck the algorithm," I said. "Just tell us about your findings."

"Well, here it is, gentlemen. On Rick's suggestion, I looked at any contact with Islam that the women may have had. It wasn't easy. My team and I interviewed dozens of family members and colleagues. The hypothesis behind our study was revenge, that radicals may have sought revenge on enemies of Islam. Here's the bottom line. Of the 200 women in the study, every one of them has written or spoken negatively about radical Islam. In the case of Rick's wife, Ellen, she actually killed an al-Qaeda big shot. And Admiral Ashley Patterson once sank an Iranian ship."

Joe Flynn went on for 45 minutes, victim by victim, citing speeches or emails or articles that came from the women victims. Every single woman had at some point expressed a negative opinion of Islam, or, in the case of Ellen and Admiral Patterson, actually engaged in combat with an Islamic force.

"Holy shit," said Buster, "we have a target profile."

"Joe, I thank you very much. I'm going to put a commendation in your file, and I'll make sure Director Auletta sees it. Great job. You can go now."

"Are you sure you don't want me to explain how I derived the algorithm."

"No, we're good to go for now, Joe. Thanks again."

I hate to cut a guy off when he wants to show us his hard work. He was proud of what he'd done and he had every right to be; but we had a lot of ground to cover, and listening to geek speak would only slow us down.

"So, guys, we have a working hypothesis for a target profile: a relatively young prominent woman who has had a negative interaction with Islam, either by opinion or action."

"Big question," said Bennie. "Why are they just targeting women?"

"The answer to that is we don't know. But it may have something to do with the creepy inner workings of the jihadi mind. They think of women as servants, as chattel. When they see a strong woman, such as Ellen, they lash out. When Ellen shot that guy, he was in the process of torturing one of the other female hostages."

"We can't assume that they won't expand their target list," said Buster. "The fact that they've narrowed their targets could mean that the substance can't be manufactured on a large scale, so they focus their hits to conserve their weapon supply."

# CHAPTER THIRTY-TWO

"Rick, it's Barbara. Director Watson's in New York and wants to have a meeting at 2 p.m. Please call Buster. She wants to meet with him too."

FBI Director Sarah Watson has a well-deserved reputation for starting meetings on time, so the two of us walked into Barbara's office five minutes early. Watson can get testy as hell when anybody's late for a meeting.

"I think the director has some important stuff to talk about," said Auletta.

Two o'clock came and went. The three of us reviewed recent events and made some preliminary notes.

"Elsie, it's Barbara." said Auletta over the intercom to her assistant. "Have you seen Director Watson? She was supposed to be in my office for a meeting over a half-hour ago."

"Wow, that's unlike her."

"I agree, Elsie. See if you can find her."

It was now 3 p.m., a full hour after the time Watson had set for the meeting.

We heard a knock on the door. Elsie, Barbara's assistant, led Director Watson into the room. From behind Watson's back, Elsie shrugged her shoulders, raised her eyelids, and held her hands in front of her, palms up, the universal sign for "What the hell is going on?"

Watson walked over to a chair along the wall.

"Madam Director," said Barbara, "please sit at the head of the table."

Watson walked over and took her place. She looked at each of us for a few moments.

"Hi, Mickey," she said to me. "Hello, Alma," she said to Barbara. "Hi, Bruiser," she said to Buster.

She sat at the head of the table and kept smiling at the three of us. A few seconds went by, probably just moments, but it seemed like an hour.

"So what are you folks doing here? This is *my* office."

After the events of the past few weeks, including my wife and then the First Lady coming down with *The Syndrome*, the three of us started diagnosing what our eyes and ears showed us. Holy shit, I thought, the Director of the FBI has gotten *The Syndrome*.

"Okay, get out of here," Watson screamed loudly, "get the fuck out of here, *now.*"

FBI and CIA agents are trained for the unexpected. We're trained how to cope with challenging situations, and how to meet a surprise with a quick decision and move on. But none of us knew how to handle this one. We were loudly ordered to leave Barbara Auletta's office, by a woman who thought the office was hers.

"Sure thing, Sarah," said Auletta. "Come on, guys, let's go." Barbara is one cool operator.

"Bennie," Barbara said into her phone as we stepped into the hallway, "I've got a situation for you. Bring two security people with you and meet me outside my office."

That evening, FBI Director Sarah Watson, age 42, one of the most powerful officials in the federal government, was admitted to the psychiatric wing of Bellevue Hospital, heavily sedated because of her agitation.

# CHAPTER THIRTY-THREE

"My fellow Americans," began President Reynolds, "the past month has seen a dramatic increase in reported cases of a terrible disease, a disease that appears to be Alzheimer's. What's different about the statistics that we're seeing is the profile of the people afflicted. We're accustomed to thinking of Alzheimer's as an affliction of the elderly, but what we've seen recently is a sharp rise in cases of early-onset dementia. The profile is clear. Younger women, no older than 42, have succumbed to this disease in alarming numbers. As you all know, my own wife, Amanda Reynolds, the First Lady, has become a victim. Amanda is 41 years old." He stopped to take a sip of water. This guy is tough under stress, I thought.

"I've just been informed that Sarah Watson, Director of the FBI, has come down with the condition. She's 42 years old. People have speculated that, because of the profile of the victims, these incidents may be some kind of deliberate act. We have no hard evidence of any such thing, but we're not taking any leads off the table. At this point, we're not even certain that the disease is

Alzheimer's, or something that mimics its symptoms. We are calling the affliction simply *The Syndrome.*"

He took a deep breath.

"A few months ago, you heard me announce from this very podium that World War III has begun. Whether we are seeing another horrible front in that war is something I cannot answer today. But we're not taking a wait-and-see attitude. Today, I have appointed Doctor Frank Buchannan, one of the nation's top epidemiologists, to head up a massive study at the Centers for Disease Control. Doctor Buchannan is a medical detective. With his team, he will look at every possible clue to solve this crisis. And yes, it is a crisis. Our nation is losing scores of young, talented women. Together we will stop this scourge. Thank you, and God bless America."

⇒⊹ ⊹⇐

"Perfect, just perfect," Buster said.

"Do you think he went too heavy on the deliberate act theory?" said Bennie.

"I don't think so," I said. "Reynolds knows what he's doing. You can't turn on a news show without seeing some talking head speculating that the incidents may have been intentional. If Reynolds didn't touch on the deliberate act theory, nobody would believe him. But he didn't go anywhere near the spray bottles. That will come out soon. Also, appointing Frank Buchannan to head up the effort is a great call. He couldn't have picked a better man."

"Another good thing that will come from this," said Buster, "will be call-in advice to the CDC from self-appointed mavens. Remember that book by Malcolm Gladwell, *The Tipping Point?* In the book, he talks about the power of mavens. He wrote that a certain hand soap actually had an 800 phone number imprinted on it. It was a 'maven trap.' He said that may seem ridiculous, but the marketing idea was to encourage 'soap mavens' to weigh in. With the prevalence of Alzheimer's, Frank Buchannan and his team will have lots of help from self-appointed experts across the country."

"The spray bottle idea will have to become public soon," I said. "I'd love to see what the mavens will have to say about that."

# CHAPTER THIRTY-FOUR

I got home to our apartment, *our* apartment, later than usual at 9:30. I'm using work to keep my sanity. When I walked in, the first thing I noticed was silence. Dead, fucking silence. Not a bright, cheery, beautiful woman who would throw her arms around my neck and kiss me, but silence. I made myself a cup of green tea and sat in front of the TV, the TV that Ellen had stared at blankly. I've got to stop this shit, I reminded myself. I'm in a position where I can be of some use to my country. I can be of some use to the future women who may come down with *The Syndrome*. I can make a difference. I can kill a few fucking people. Okay, stop! This way of thinking will go nowhere good.

I clicked off the TV and I tried to read a book. I have no idea what I was reading. Thank God I was feeling tired, because I sure as hell needed some sleep. I walked into the guest bedroom. No way in hell could I stand the thought of sleeping in the bed that I shared with Ellen.

Bennie, God bless him, was helping me to get through this shit. As he always reminded me, don't force out negative thoughts.

Let them in and look at them, and they'll go away by themselves. But the one big negative thought never seemed to go away—I may never see my Ellen again. It's more than just a thought, it's becoming more like a condition that I live through, something that consumes me like chronic pain. It's just there.

I clicked on the TV again, probably a dumb move to make right before going to bed. As per Ellen's plan, I thought of a Jerry Seinfeld joke before I turned on the TV. It wasn't funny.

"Wolf Blitzer reporting for CNN, ladies and gentlemen. We've found out from the President's address to the nation that Sarah Watson, the Director of the FBI, has come down with the terrible affliction that's attacking women, a condition known as *The Syndrome.*

"The White House has just announced that Barbara Auletta, the Director of the New York office of the FBI, has been appointed as the new provisional FBI Director.

"FBI Agent Rick Bellamy, the former head of the New York Counterterrorism office, has been named as Barbara Auletta's replacement as Director of the New York FBI headquarters. The White House also announced that the New York office will be in charge of nationwide counterterrorism efforts.

"You may recall that Agent Bellamy's wife came down with *The Syndrome* a few weeks ago. She is under care in a nursing home.

"In other news…"

Blitzer didn't have to remind me that my Ellen lives in a nursing home.

# CHAPTER THIRTY-FIVE

"There's a guy named Mike B. on the phone for you, Rick. He wouldn't give his last name."

When Imam Muhammed Busharif (Mike B.) calls, I drop everything.

"Mike, what's up?"

"I gotta see you, Rick. Central Park at noon?"

"You got it, Mike. I'll bring Buster."

＝＋＋＝

Buster and I walked to Bethesda Terrace, the restaurant near Bethesda Fountain in Central Park, our usual meeting place when we see Imam Mike. It's been a few weeks since Ellen moved into the nursing home, shortly after she came down with *The Syndrome* on April 4. For the rest of my days, I'll think of life as two distinct phases, before and after that horrible April 4.

It was a warm day, so I told Mike to meet us at the outdoor café. As usual, we had a hard time spotting Mike. Under Buster's coaching, Mike had become a master of disguises. We saw a guy in a softball uniform wearing dark sunglasses. He brushed his hand across the peak of his cap, a sign to let us know it was him. We walked over and sat at his table.

"Mike," I said, "your call to me at the White House blew the doors off everything. Your spray bottle information has moved us forward by miles. I'd like to personally introduce you to President Reynolds someday, but that's not likely to happen soon. So, my friend, what's on your mind today?"

"Rick, before I go any further, I want to tell you again how sorry I am about your wife. To think that the scumbag who did this calls himself a Muslim makes my skin crawl. But my job is to feed you guys information, and I have some big stuff to talk about."

"Any more on the water bottles, Mike?" asked Buster.

"Yes, a lot. From what I've been picking up, whatever shit they're putting into those bottles can only be produced in small amounts. But that will change a few weeks from now. They have a plant in Baltimore, and I'm guessing it's a manufacturing facility of some sort. I've been hearing a lot of Arabic words that can best be translated as 'ramp up.' "

Buster asked him the Arabic word. When Mike told him, he said, "Yes, 'ramp up' is a perfect translation."

"So they're looking to make a lot of this spray bottle stuff, whatever it is, and they're looking to make it in large amounts. These assholes seem to think that they can shoot their mouths off in my mosque and nobody will notice. There's been a lot of giggling about 'hundreds of infidel bitches.' You know how these creeps revel in depravity."

"Mike, I'm sure I know the answer or else you would have told us already, but do you have any idea where this Baltimore facility is?"

"I can't give you an address, but I hear a lot of talk about an aquarium. I checked online and found that there's a National

Aquarium in Baltimore. One bastard even talked about making a lot of fish forgetful. That's as much as I know about a location at this point, but I'll keep listening."

"Do you have the names of the men you've overheard, Mike?" asked Buster.

"Sure. Here are their names and addresses. Just don't tell them I sent you."

"Mike," said Buster, "you're turning into a top-level spook. If you ever decide to change professions, I'd love to personally sponsor you into the CIA."

"I think I'm more valuable where I am."

"Very true, Mike. Hey, while we're on the subject, keep your head down. If you get yourself whacked, it won't do you, your family, or America any good."

"Don't worry, Buster. I'll continue to parrot my mild denunciation of terror every time I hear about another job these slimeballs pull off."

"Anything else you can think of, Mike?" I said.

"Yeah. They're on to you about the tracking devices on the surface-to-air missiles. They know that you have drones patrolling runways."

"Mike, neither Rick nor myself told you anything about tracking devices on the missiles."

"You didn't have to. I heard it in my mosque. Here are the names of the guys I heard talking about it. I'll let you know if I hear anything more about the exact location of that place in Baltimore."

# CHAPTER THIRTY-SIX

"A Mr. MacPherson is on the line for you, Rick."

"Hello, Rick, it's Angus MacPherson, lad. I need to see you."

Angus MacPherson, one of the wealthiest men in America, was Ellen's biggest client. Last year, MacPherson's wife and daughter were kidnapped, along with Ellen, as part of an al-Qaeda plot to destroy five shopping malls that MacPherson had planned. Ellen saved the life of his daughter, Jane, and he now refers to Ellen as his adopted daughter. He was the first person to visit Ellen after she was admitted to New Horizons. Angus is a charming Scotsman and a brilliant businessman. He's also a good friend.

"Angus, it's good to hear from you. I need to get out of here for a bit, so I'll meet you in your office."

MacPherson International headquarters is on Park Avenue, about 25 minutes from my office. When I arrived, his secretary immediately showed me in. His office is what you would expect of a major real estate developer. About 30 by 40 feet, the mahogany walls framed the place with opulence. A large table off to the side was covered with plans and blueprints. The floor was polished mahogany, with a large Persian rug in the middle. Angus walked from around his desk and gave me a bear hug. He has a large jovial face that is usually lit up by a broad smile. But his face told me that he was upset about something.

"They've done it to Jane, lad. They've given her the sickness, just like they gave it to Ellen. At the age of 26, Jane's mind is leaving her." He broke down into sobs.

"Where is Jane now, Angus?"

"She's at my house in Scarsdale with 24-hour nursing care. Rick, she barely knows my name, and she thinks that my wife, Margo, is her sister. They tried to kill the poor lass before, but Ellen saved her life. Now, there's nobody to save either of them."

"So you and I are part of the growing brotherhood of people who have lost important women in their lives, Angus. I know what you're going through, my friend. Is there anything I can do?"

"I'm sure you FBI folks are on top of this, but I want you to know that my other business, MacPherson Security, is back in action. I've rooted out all of the Islamic infiltrators, with no small amount of help from you FBI people. It's now a fully functional security company, manned with some of the best people I could find. I'm looking to kill some bastards, lad, as I'm sure you understand."

"Of course I understand, Angus, but please don't go off on a personal vendetta, as reasonable as that may be. Do you think that I'm not looking for blood? I am, but I know that the way we're going to fight this goddam war is to use our brains, not our guts—or our anger. Ellen has been turned into a zombie, and I'm looking to find who did it. But the only way we can do that is to move carefully."

"Can you tell me where you are in the investigation, Rick? Are you in any way close to finding a solution?"

"Angus, as you understand, I can't tell you everything that I know, but I can tell you that we're a lot closer now than we were a week ago. We know that *The Syndrome* is caused by a deliberate act.

We're pretty sure it has something to do with a substance that's sprayed into a person's face with a water bottle. We also know that the jihadis are planning to ramp up production of whatever the substance is. But our biggest problem is just that—we don't know what it is that they're spraying into women's faces. How was Jane attacked?"

"As she walked into her office, a window washer sprayed her. A friend who was with her told me how it happened. The man apologized, claiming that it was an accident. Jane thought nothing more about it. She started to show symptoms the next day."

"That's exactly what happened to Ellen. Something so simple, so apparently harmless. But to get back to what I was saying, please don't go off on your own, Angus. Leave it to the pros. And please keep something in mind: the White House is all over this like flies on sugar. I hate to say it, but the attack on Amanda Reynolds could be the best thing this case has going for it. You heard the president on TV. He's appointed some great people to track this from the Centers for Disease Control. It's just a matter of time."

"Even if they crack the case, Rick, what do you think that will do for Jane and Ellen?"

"I have no idea, Angus."

"I have one word for you, lad, and I'd like your thoughts on it."

"So what's the word?"

"Baltimore."

Holy shit! If I wanted to keep that a secret, I was afraid that my face blew it.

"You've heard about a facility in Baltimore?"

"Yes, and my people from MacPherson Security are on the case. Don't worry, lad, I won't take this into my own hands, but you won't mind some investigative help, would you?"

"I'm supposed to say no, Angus, but I trust you. We have a lead that it may be located near the national aquarium. Do you have any thoughts on that?"

"Yes, it is near the aquarium. I assume you have the area under satellite surveillance."

"You know I can't confirm that, Angus."

"I'll take that as a yes, lad. I will feed you whatever information we gather, Rick. So now you have MacPherson Security helping you, along with Imam Busharif."

"You know about Mike?"

"As I said, we have good people working at MacPherson."

⊷⊶

After my meeting with Angus, I went to New Horizons to see Ellen.

"Hi, Rick, good to see you," said Nurse Nancy. "I have some great news for you. Come to Ellen's room and I'll let you see for yourself."

Ellen was laughing, laughing out loud. I wanted to pick her up and hug her, but I didn't want to interfere with her joy. She was watching TV, laughing hysterically, and occasionally clapping her hands.

"We've found something that makes her happy, Rick."

I looked at the TV. Barney the dinosaur was going through his antics on the kiddie show, *Barney and Friends*, along with a bunch of other goofy characters. Barney the dinosaur made Ellen happy.

"With a great big hug and a kiss from me to you, won't you say you love me too," said the purple freak with a weird squeaky voice.

"Hey, Rick, smile. Aren't you happy to see Ellen enjoying herself?"

"Nancy, let me tell you a few things about Ellen that you may not know. She has an undergraduate degree in architecture from MIT. She then went to Wharton where she got an MBA. *Architectural Digest* magazine picked her as Architect of the Year in 2014. She's written two books on modern architecture, one of which was a complicated mathematical treatise. The other book is on *The New*

121

*York Times* Best Seller List. She and I are working on a novel together, but, of course, that project is on hold. And you expect me to be happy that she enjoys watching a stupid fucking dinosaur show?"

"Rick, I've learned over the years working with dementia patients that you take small victories and welcome them. Now park your ass on the chair next to her and enjoy the show, the stupid fucking dinosaur show, as you call it."

# CHAPTER THIRTY-SEVEN

"Rick, it's Buster. There's a guy you need to meet. He'll be here at two this afternoon."

"What's he all about?"

"All I can tell you is that he's the most talented man I ever met when it comes to tracing money, and what goes on behind the money."

※ ※

A guy wearing the most expensive Savile Row suit I'd ever seen walked into Buster's office.

"Rick, meet Trevor McMartin. Trevor's a bank examiner from Australia. He's been hired by our friend Angus MacPherson. Trevor's also done a lot of work for the CIA. Angus called and suggested we get together. I've worked with Trevor before, and I've been amazed at his money tracking skills."

"G'day, mates. Pleasure to meet you, Rick. Long time no see, Buster (*Bustah*)."

"I've briefed Trevor on our investigation, including the spray bottles. I'll let him fill us in on what he's up to."

"Let me start off by saying how sorry I am to hear about your wife, Rick. Angus MacPherson's daughter, as you know, just came down with this thing you call *The Syndrome* as well."

I thanked him for his kind words.

"The first observation I want to share with you blokes is the money involved in radical Islamist operations since the start of this whole mess on 10/15. These bastards are swimming in money, and a lot of it comes from ISIS and its oil revenues. They also take in a lot of income by selling the American assets they've stolen in Iraq. Except for the occasional train or building bombings, some of their operations are expensive to pull off. Many of the jobs require a lot of men and a lot of payroll, and both ISIS and al-Qaeda have the money to burn. As you know, they also have an unending supply of young people willing to commit suicide."

"Trevor," I said, "please bring me up to speed on how you track money and how that links with terrorist activities."

"Sure, Rick. Your Aussie friend is a bit of a computer whiz, if I do say so myself."

"He's a fucking genius, Rick," said Buster. "Sorry, Trevor, please continue."

"I always enjoy a compliment, mate. I've developed a number of computer algorithms that send up flags whenever a substantial amount of money goes from one place to another. Then I look to see how the money is spent. There's been more money laid out on hazardous material suits and paraphernalia than I've ever seen. There is also a huge amount of being spent on chemicals of all sorts. And how's this: I could never imagine such a large amount of funds being spent on humble water spray bottles, the apparent weapon of choice for crippling those poor women."

"But how can you tell what the money is being used for?" I said. "I'm sure they're not stupid enough to use credit cards. They probably pay cash."

"Rick, it would take me all day to explain that, but let me assure you, my algorithm can track how many sticks of gum you chew in a day."

"Trevor, can you track the money to specific locations?" I asked.

"It's always a question of cash flowing from one location to another. Most of the funds that I've tracked recently originate in a bank in Yemen, and most wind up clearing through Bank of America, if you can enjoy the irony."

"And what location on earth seems to bother your algorithm the most?"

"Baltimore."

# CHAPTER THIRTY-EIGHT

Melanie Copeland walked down Fifth Avenue hand in hand with her fiancé, Derek Richardson, a linebacker with the New York Giants. They walked toward the entrance to 30 Rockefeller Plaza, where Melanie had just begun her new job as a reporter with NBC News. At the age of 29, she considered herself lucky to land such a prized spot. Melanie had recently written an article about Islamic terrorism that was published in *The Atlantic*. In the article, she complained about the silence of the Muslim clergy in face of the constant terrorist attacks. "The sound of silence can be the sound of cowardice," she wrote.

In the article, she also discussed her recent trip to Afghanistan. While there, a local woman she had befriended told her that a stoning would occur in the village soccer field one afternoon. The thought sickened her, but the journalist in her forced her to go as a witness. Dressed in a full burqa, Melanie watched "the ceremony." According to people she interviewed, a young woman, age 19, was sentenced to be stoned to death. The offense for which she was convicted after a 20-minute trial was being raped by three young men. She couldn't believe that a woman could be sentenced to death for having a vicious crime committed *against her*. She interviewed a total of 10 villagers, including a local imam, who all corroborated the story—the woman would be executed because she was found to have acted "provocatively" by having her legs exposed.

As was the custom, the convicted woman was buried up to her chest in a standing position. The subhead in the article read, "Savagery in a Soccer Stadium." She wrote about the apparent glee of the men throwing the death stones at the woman. Her editor at *The Atlantic* suggested that she turn down the heat of her words, but Melanie insisted that he go with the draft as written. About a month after the article was published, Melanie changed her email address, Twitter, and Facebook accounts because she was tired of the constant death threats.

A man was washing the windows of the building entrance as they walked toward the door. He turned his spray bottle toward Melanie's face. With the instant reflexes of a veteran NFL linebacker, Derek drove a fist into the man's face, dropping him to the pavement. John McGuinness, a nearby policeman, saw the melee and ran to the scene, gun drawn.

"Don't touch that bottle," McGuinness yelled. He had read the All-Points Bulletin that morning that all police officers should be on the lookout for men wielding spray bottles. He reached into his pocket and withdrew a plastic evidence bag along with pliers he carried with him. As the bulletin had recommended, he carefully lifted the bottle with his pliers and placed it into the bag. McGuinness called for assistance as he put handcuffs on the still unconscious window washer.

As McGuiness took statements from Melanie and Derek, an SUV with the words Columbia Presbyterian Disease Control Unit pulled next to the curb. Tyrone Mackle, a medical technician and assistant to Dr. Frank Buchannan, reached into the back of the vehicle and withdrew a Styrofoam box. He picked up the evidence bag containing the bottle and placed it into the box.

"Did any liquid escape the bottle?" Mackle shouted.

"The only liquid that escaped around here was the blood from that scumbag's nose," said Derek the linebacker.

As Mackle was about to put the box into his car, McGuinness yelled, "Hey, pal, that's evidence. You're not going anywhere with it."

"I understand, officer. Please let me make a phone call so we can clear this up."

Within three minutes, a call was placed to Dr. Buchannan, who called the White House, where the Chief of Staff placed a call to the NYPD Police Commissioner, who then called McGuiness on his radio.

"You've got some serious connections, pal," said McGuinness.

"And you're going to have a glowing commendation in your record, officer."

Mackle drove away as McGuinness helped the window washer into the back of a patrol car.

Basic police work.

<hr/>

"Rick, it's Buster. We just got a big break. A window washer tried to spray a woman reporter for NBC news. Fortunately, her boyfriend is Derek Richardson, the linebacker with the Giants. Richardson clocked the guy, and the cops put the bottle in an evidence bag. It's now in the hands of Frank Buchannan."

"Where's the window washer?"

"In custody at police headquarters. I called and they understand that this is an FBI and CIA matter. I'll meet you there. You may need an Arabic translator."

"I know nothing. I am weendow washer," said Yousef Mousell.

"And what led you to believe that the young woman needed a washing?" I asked. He seemed to want to talk, which surprised both Buster and me. He didn't take his chance to lawyer up.

"I am making joke with young lady. I not making harm to her."

"What was in the bottle?"

"Water and cleaning stuff. My boss telling me be careful because cleaning stuff can sting your eyes."

"And you weren't concerned about getting the 'cleaning stuff' in the woman's eyes?"

"I not spray. I just hold bottle up to her and make joke."

"It's not a very funny joke. Who is your boss?"

"Some guy from National Cleaning Contractors. Office is on 32nd Street."

"I'll check it out," said Buster as he went into the next room to make a call.

My cell phone rang. It was Dr. Buchannan's office.

"Rick, do not let that fucker out of your sight," yelled the gentle intellectual Dr. Frank Buchannan, dropping an uncharacteristic *f-bomb.* "We've just started testing, but I can tell you that the contents of the bottle is definitely not any kind of cleaning solution. We don't know what it is yet, but we know what it's not."

"Bless you, Frank. Call me when you find out anything," I said as I unwrapped a Maalox.

Buster came back into the room.

"They confirmed that the guy works for them. It's a good thing I speak Arabic."

"Why?"

"The boss man sounds like he's from Afghanistan. This may be a bigger lead than we thought, not that I would ever profile somebody."

"Did you tell the boss man anything about what's going on?"

"Hey, Rick, what kind of spook do I look like? I told him that I was a doctor and Mousell was in a car accident and couldn't talk."

⇒⊢ ⊣⇐

"You and I need to relax a bit, Buster. I hear there's a terrific aquarium in Baltimore. We've got to locate that factory. How about you and I head there tomorrow?"

"Great idea, Rick. I'll call and make plane arrangements."

"Plane? I thought we'd take a road trip. We have a lot of things we can go over in the car."

"But why not fly, Rick?"

"Do *you* want to fly? The airlines are running on a shoestring schedule, and it takes a couple of days to reserve the FBI Gulfstream."

"Actually, a car sounds like a great idea. It's only about three hours or so to Baltimore."

Buster and I were bullshitting each other. Two tough guys didn't want to come right out and say that we were afraid to fly.

# CHAPTER THIRTY-NINE

We drove to the Baltimore FBI office where we met a driver assigned to us. We agreed that we didn't want the distraction of one of us driving a car. Our driver, Don Frankel, was an FBI agent. He had been briefed on the sensitive and Top Secret nature of the investigation.

"Let me see those satellite photos again, Buster."

Buster handed me a few photos that were snapped from the sky.

"We see a lot of coming and going to this building," Buster said as he pointed to the structure on the photos. "This place gets a lot of package deliveries of all different sizes. The address is 128 Walton Street."

"Don, plug that address into your GPS."

The building, right down the block from the National Aquarium, looked like any small industrial structure. It could be used as a distribution facility—or a factory.

"Pull over and park across the street, Don. We're going to do a little old-fashioned surveillance."

We sat for two hours, snapping pictures and recording what we saw. Five deliveries in two hours, and ten different men entering or leaving.

"I didn't see one beard or even a turban, Buster. This place could be a Knights of Columbus Hall."

"Remember, Rick. The new face of terror is home grown, and they've learned to lurk in the shadows. The latest newly hatched jihadis that we have on our database don't use their Muslim names, don't have beards, and don't wear religious clothing. They don't go to mosques, and they don't visit radical websites. Their new pattern is to fly below our radar. They live in the shadows of terror."

As if to confirm what Buster had just said, a man yelled to another as he approached the building. "Ali, may peace be upon you." I thought the other guy was going to punch him. The other man shouted, "Shut up. What have you been told about using our Muslim names?" Obviously, they didn't notice the three of us sitting in the car. Tinted windows are a great invention, I thought, especially for surveillance.

"What we just heard, Rick, was a man shouting the new protocols of jihad."

"Check out the roofline," said Don Frankel as he snapped photos. "I count four security lights just on this side of the building alone. And look at the security cameras mounted at the corners. This is no food distribution plant."

"Well, we don't have anything that would hold up in a court of law, but I think we've narrowed our focus to 128 Walton Street. What do you think, Buster?"

"Now if we could just figure out what the hell they're doing."

# CHAPTER FORTY

"Wanna throw up?" said Bennie as we walked into Barbara Auletta's office for a meeting.

"Not really, Ben, if it's all the same to you. What would make us throw up?"

"Are you guys dog lovers like me?" said Bennie.

Barbara, Buster and I nodded. I don't own a dog, but I like them.

"Check out this flash video that we liberated from that window washer's workbag."

Bennie gave it to Barbara, who plugged it into her computer and swung around the monitor for us to see.

A man, without a trace of an accent, was playing with a yellow Labrador puppy. "Fritzie," the man yelled, and the dog responded by approaching and wagging his tail.

"Where's George?" the man said. Fritzie ran across the room and put his paw on the lap of another man, presumably George. The guy then put three objects on the floor. They looked like dog treats. "Where's the chicken?" said the man. Fritzie went for the treat to the left. Obviously, this guy was an experienced dog trainer.

"Now comes the funny part," announced the guy named George. He then sprayed a water bottle into Fritzie's face, saying, "Enjoy The Scent of Revenge." Fritzie shook his head, his ears flapping in protest.

The scene faded to black. This guy knows how to make a video, I thought. He's also a sadistic scumbag.

"It's now three days later," announced the training guy to the videocam, barely able to contain his glee. "Fritzie, come here."

The dog looked at him with that face of confusion when a dog doesn't know what's going on.

"Where's George, Fritzie?"

No response at all from the dog, other than its head tilted to the side and his ears cocked. His tail was dead still, not the normal excited wagging of a Labrador puppy.

"Where's the chicken?" asked the trainer, as he put three morsels on the floor. The dog ran and ate all three, resulting in a vicious kick to its stomach from George, which the trainer found hysterically funny.

"It gets better," said the man to the videocam. "The next scene will be three days from now."

Fritzie lay on the floor with his tongue out. The trainer repeatedly called his name, which resulted in no response from the dog. The operator of the videocam showed a close-up of the dog's face as the trainer said, "Where's the chicken?"

I never knew that a dog was capable of what we call a "vacant stare," but there it was. Words, or even food, did not register with the poor animal. He lay on the floor, as the trainer shouted, "Bad dog." With that, he cracked a baseball bat across Fritzie's head. All three men in the room laughed hysterically as the dog lay motionless, apparently dead.

"We've just seen a jihadi training video," said Bennie. "That poor dog was a rehearsal prop for attacks on young women."

# CHAPTER FORTY-ONE

"How's Sarah doing?" I asked the new FBI Director Barbara Auletta.

"I visited her this morning. Rick, I understand what you're going through with Ellen. To answer your question, Sarah Watson is doing terribly. She didn't know who I was, of course, but the worst part is that she doesn't recognize any of her nurses or assistants. She's extremely agitated and aggressive. Her doctor told me that they have to sedate her more than any other dementia patient he's ever worked with. Sarah is one of the smartest people I've ever known. Now she's reduced to a tantrum-throwing toddler."

"Imagine how I feel when I visit Ellen and find her watching a children's show on TV. The only thing she enjoys is Barney the dinosaur."

"Rick, I'm not telling you something that you don't already know. We've got to find a way to put an end to these attacks."

"Madam Director—"

"Call me Barbara for chrissake."

"Barbara, you and I are law enforcement people. We're used to weighing evidence, but mainly we're used to taking action. Problem is, it's out of our hands. Hell, it's out of the president's hands. We think we've isolated that factory in Baltimore, which is a good breakthrough, but it will only answer part of the question. If we take out Baltimore, we'll prevent mass manufacturing of whatever the substance is, but we won't be able to stop a lone actor with a spray bottle in his hand. Whether we like it or not, the fate of future victims is in the hands of doctors and scientists."

"Until they make a big discovery, all the hell we can do is watch talented young women cheering on Barney the dinosaur," Barbara said.

# CHAPTER FORTY-TWO

Joan Paddington, age 39, was the founder and CEO of Megasoft, one of the largest software companies in the country. She was in the boardroom of Goldman Sachs to discuss the upcoming initial public offering, or IPO, to bring Megasoft public. The business news had been lighting up like a switchboard about the move. Most analysts expected it to be the largest IPO since Facebook. One of the biggest assets of Megasoft was Paddington herself. She was to Megasoft what Steve Jobs was to Apple.

She founded the company at the age of 25, not surprising in the youthful world of high technology. *Forbes* magazine once referred to her as "pure energy." In the male-dominated industry of Silicon Valley, Paddington was a legend. With strategic acquisitions and brilliant marketing, she put her company on a pedestal. Like any dominant figure in business, she wasn't without controversy. Although it was never proven, it was well known among insiders that Paddington refused to hire Muslims. An anonymous source was cited, quoting Paddington, "I don't want any of my employees taking time off from work to spread a rug and pray."

George Morgan, CEO of Goldman Sachs, sat at the head of the table. A dozen employees of Goldman Sachs were at the meeting, most of whom were stock analysts. Three vice presidents of Megasoft were on hand, seated next to Paddington.

"Joan, it's a delight to have you here with us today. I'd be less than honest if I said that we aren't excited about your upcoming IPO. You've built one hell of a company, and soon you'll be a billionaire, which you well deserve. Our valuation numbers look fabulous, and I think the market will fall in love with this stock. A few of our folks have some questions for you."

"Why?"

Everyone laughed, assuming Paddington was making a casual joke.

"That's a good question, Joan. Our people have been pouring over your books like fleas on a fox. But hey, stock analysts all over the world are going to have questions, so I figured we'd give you some practice."

"Who are you?"

Only a couple of people chuckled. Paddington looked serious when she asked Morgan who he was.

"I'm George Morgan, your key to a gigantic bank vault," he said with a smile.

"I forgot my umbrella."

"But it's not raining, Joan."

"Maybe it will. Where's my goddam umbrella?" she said loudly.

Jack Levine, the senior analyst at Goldman, ignored the umbrella comments and decided to start asking questions.

"Joan, we've noticed that your European sales have slowed over the past two quarters. Would you like to comment?"

"Fuck 'em. We can sell our shit right here."

The room was silent, except for some nervous paper shuffling.

Joan Paddington sat back in her chair, lowered her chin, and fell asleep, snoring loudly.

⊷⊶

That afternoon, Joan Paddington was admitted to Bellevue Hospital in Manhattan. A week later, suffering from advanced dementia, she took up residence in the San Jose Nursing Facility near her home in California. The Megasoft IPO was delayed indefinitely.

# CHAPTER FORTY-THREE

F BI Director Auletta, Buster, and I met in Barbara's New York
office with our Australian bank examiner friend Trevor
McMartin. Trevor had requested the meeting.

"I've never seen anything like this, folks. In all my years examining business transactions, I have to admit I'm stupefied."

"Does this have anything to do with Baltimore, Trevor?" I asked.

"It's a lot bigger than just one location, mate. The subject I want
to talk to you folks about today is ISIS, and its vast wealth. Ever
since the constant terrorist attacks began on 10/15, a lot of people,
myself included, have wondered how the jihadis are able to carry
on such a relentless series of attacks, both big and small. Attacks
like these can't happen without money, lots of money. Especially
since they've started recruiting what you call home-grown radicals,
the pattern is clear. We've noticed this in Australia too. Think of
the world of radical Islam as a business. I know that sounds absurd,
but hear me out. The frequency of the attacks requires a lot of people. They need planners, bomb makers, as well as the actors themselves. In other words, ISIS and al-Qaeda are high employment

businesses. High employment means payroll, a big payroll. Now it's no longer a ragtag operation with low-skilled players. It's a vast and complex organization."

"Why are we seeing such a large influx of money to the radicals, Trevor?" asked Barbara Auletta.

"In the past few years, things have changed, Madam Director. ISIS now controls a large part of Syria, Iraq, and surrounding countries making up the Levant. Again, getting back to my business analogy, put yourself in the position of a stock analyst, which is exactly the way I operate. A good analyst would recommend investing, so to speak, in Jihad, Inc., for two main reasons: acquisitions and sales. First are the acquisitions. Because of their ongoing land grabs, their conquests have included vast physical assets. I'm talking about American military equipment and weapons that were left behind, as well as oil industry infrastructure. Even though the price of oil is down recently, the black gold provides a steady flow of cash. Beyond the physical assets, they have also plundered millions from banks. So that's the acquisitions part of the business. They grow by acquiring assets.

"The second part of their success has to do with sales. What do they sell? Death, or more exactly, the fear of death. You only need to turn on the telly to learn about the latest kidnapping ransom demand. If the ransom isn't paid, as we all know, some poor bloke will lose his head, or worse. Remember that Jordanian pilot who they burned alive? Most of the big countries refuse to pay the ransoms, but that doesn't stop their sales from being brisk."

"Are ransom demands actually being satisfied?" asked Buster.

"Well get this, mate. *The New York Times* reported on a few of their ransom successes. France paid out the most to al-Qaeda affiliates, about $58 million. The next-highest payout was $20 million from Oman and Qatar. Switzerland paid out $12 million, Spain $11 million, and Austria $3 million in the same time frame. That's $104 million, over just six years. Yes, folks, sales are humming. We may see Japan refusing to pay a huge ransom demand, but there are a bunch of willing ransom payers standing behind every one who declines. The money that the radicals make from acquisitions and ransom sales funds a big payroll, and don't forget R&D. We still don't know what's behind the strange substance that's taking down the young women, but you can be sure it wasn't made in some garage with a chemistry set."

"So we've been operating on the assumption that we're dealing with a bunch of sheep herders," said Barbara Auletta, "but you're saying that our enemy is wealthy and sophisticated and ready to use the wealth to kill us."

"Madam Director, you've summarized it perfectly."

# CHAPTER FORTY-FOUR

"Rick, it's Mike Busharif. I need to see you. How about the usual place, the Bethesda Terrace in Central Park?"

Every time I meet Imam Mike, besides the valuable information he gives me, I look forward to seeing his latest disguise. Mike is beginning to love his status as a spy.

I walked into the Bethesda Terrace restaurant. It was mid-May and the weather was perfect, so we agreed to sit at one of the outside tables. The hostess brought me to a table by the fountain. I scanned the diners, looking for Mike.

A tall woman with long blond hair, wearing a tasteful blue dress, approached my table. She seemed to have a tough time walking in her high heels.

"Looking for company, handsome?"

I spit my club soda across the table. She was Mike.

Mike sat down and cracked his knuckles. Our waitress came to the table to take our orders. She looked at Mike, smiling, but with frowning eyes. Mike put on his best falsetto imitation of a woman's voice and ordered a cheeseburger and a Michelob. I ordered the same.

"Rick, I think I have something that could be important. I've been hearing a lot of chatter about this, and something tells me it's for real."

"Anything to do with water bottles?" I asked.

"Yeah, it could have everything to do with water bottles. There's a guy from Chechnya named Dmitri Pushkin. He's a chemical engineer by trade and a professor at Chechen State University in Grozny. Every jihadi I've heard mention him refers to the guy as 'the chemist.' He's definitely a radical Islamist from what I've been able to find out. He's been connected in a bunch of terrorist attacks in Russia, all involving some sort of chemical substance. But here's the big thing: I've counted six times that I've heard his name in the same sentence as water bottles. Four of those times also included the phrase 'infidel bitches.' Here's a photo of the guy. I found it on the Internet on the Chechen University website."

"I assume that he resides in Chechnya, which sucks, because we sure as hell don't have any kind of extradition treaty with them."

"He's taken up a new temporary residence, Rick."

"Where?"

"Baltimore."

⊷ ⊶

"Buster, it's Rick. My office, please."

It's great that Buster's regular office has been changed from CIA Headquarters in Langley, Virginia, to the FBI office in Manhattan. Having a spy on call is a gift.

"Buster, I didn't say what you're about to hear."

"You're turning into a real spook, Rick. What's up?"

"Do you have experience with interviewing a suspect without a Foreign Intelligence Surveillance Court or FISA court order?"

"You mean kidnapping somebody to pump him for information?"
Buster likes to get right to the point.

"Well, kidnapping is a strong word. I was thinking more along
the lines of having an 'encouraged conversation.' "

"Who is he, where is he, and when do we grab him?"

"His name is Dmitri Pushkin. He's a chemical engineer and a
professor at Chechen State University in Grozny, Chechnya. Mike
Busharif told me all about him. Mike's sources said the guy is a
radical and has been involved in chemical attacks against Russian
targets. Here's a photo of Pushkin that Mike got off the university
website. Mike also said that he's heard Pushkin's name in the same
sentence as spray bottles or water bottles, and the phrase 'infidel
bitches.' He now resides, temporarily, in Baltimore."

"Baltimore? Holy shit! We've got to talk to this guy. From what
you just told me, we just may be able to get a FISA court order."

"Not a chance, Buster. All we could present is hearsay evidence,
because no way in hell would I put Mike in front of a FISA court.
Even if we did have Mike testify, all he would be able to relate
would also be hearsay."

"Yeah, but FISA court hearings aren't trials. They're pretty
loose with the rules of evidence, especially if the head of the New
York FBI Office makes the presentation. That would be you, Rick.
Also, I can check with immigration. I'll bet anything that the guy
doesn't have a good visa. At bare minimum, we can then have the
guy deported."

"I don't want him deported, do you?"

"You make a good point, Rick. When I read him his rights, I'll
say, 'You have a right to remain silent, and I have a right to call the
U.S. Citizen and Immigration and Naturalization Services.' When
do you want me to round up this scumbag?"

"Yesterday."

"I hear you, Rick, but all of a sudden, I'm starting to doubt this
plan."

"Why, this won't be the first clandestine operation you've ever pulled off. I bet you can get the go ahead from Director Carlini himself."

"Wait a minute; let's think this through, Rick. So we nail the guy and put him in an interrogation room. Do you expect him to say, 'Oh, you guys must want to know about the shit I put in those spray bottles. I thought you'd never ask.' No way. This guy is a radical. He thinks if we whack him, he gets to go to heaven and screw 72 virgins. How could we possibly give this guy a reason to open up to us?"

"Why not sodium pentothal, good old truth serum?" I said. "The only problem is that you need corroborative evidence to back it up. But we're not as concerned with prosecuting the guy as we are about getting scientific evidence. Remember, Doctor Buchannan and his team are totally focused on finding out what they can about the substance. They have the water bottle that we confiscated from that window washer in Manhattan, but they haven't come up with anything yet. We're looking for scientific evidence to solve a scientific problem."

"I agree," said Buster. "I'm more concerned about the science than I am about legal niceties."

"Hey, Buster, you and I are lawyers. We're overlooking something. So let's say we get information out of the guy with sodium pentothal, and the Buchannan team finds out what the substance is as a result. That's the corroborative evidence we need. Let the fucking Chechen government figure out how to extradite the man. Won't happen. A certain inhabitant of the Oval Office will take a personal interest in this case. So we arrest the prick on American soil, try him for murder, and send him to prison forever. And I know just the guy to supervise our interview."

"Bennie Weinberg?"

"Yup, Dr. Bullshit Detector himself.

"Buster, clear this with Carlini. Let's make this happen."

# CHAPTER FORTY-FIVE

My plane landed at Dulles Airport at 10:30 a.m. on May 19. Bennie Weinberg, my friend and favorite shrink, always says the most important person in the world not to bullshit is yourself. I'd be bullshitting if I said that I wasn't afraid of flying. The idea of a surface-to-air missile does nothing for one's enjoyment of a flight. The very thought of a SAM streaking toward your plane makes you want to buy a bus ticket. My plane had a capacity of 200 people, but I counted an even dozen aboard. Because of the importance of air travel, Congress had passed an emergency bailout to keep a few planes aloft.

My first meeting would be with Dr. Frank Buchannan, the guy in charge of the spray bottle investigation at the Centers for Disease Control. Buchannan asked to see me. I didn't think he sounded excited when I spoke to him, but my experience with scientific types is that they don't like to show emotion until they've solved something. I'd then meet with Barbara Auletta, the new Director of the FBI, my boss and friend.

━╬╫━

"Rick, good to see you. Please have a seat."

"Do you have any good news for me, Frank?"

"Yes and no."

Why the fuck do scientists have to be so cagey when answering a simple question?

"Let me rephrase my question, Frank. Do you have any solid information on the substance from examining the spray bottle?"

"Yes, we do. Whoever put this together was pretty sophisticated. The odd thing is that the substance itself isn't complicated. We've isolated three primary ingredients, and we have the amount of each. What we don't know, and are having a hard time figuring out, is how the substance could possibly result in *The Syndrome.*"

"What?" I said. "You've isolated the ingredients and determined the amounts, so what's the problem?"

"We've been experimenting with laboratory rats, of course. We can't, I'm sure you understand, use a human being as a subject. But we're a lot closer to an answer than we were before we got hold of that bottle."

"Frank, suppose, just suppose, that you could meet the guy who invented the substance. Just suppose, that's all I'm saying."

"Rick, assuming you have access to such a person, and further assuming that he tells the truth, that would put us over the goal line."

"Describe the goal line, Frank. Do we score if we find a preventive vaccine, or is the goal line a cure for the illness once it takes effect?"

"Rick, I don't want to raise any false hopes, especially with you, a guy who's been hit with this tragedy up-close and personal. Part of any scientific inquiry is acting on hunches. We all know the breakthroughs that have been made with vaccines. The best example is the Salk vaccine that can prevent polio. It can stop it, but it can't cure it. The same goes for other vaccines. So we'll consider the goal line a vaccine. We cross that line and we can prevent more women from being stricken. But, Rick, don't expect a cure, my friend. I hate to say that, but I want to be straight with you."

An old friend of mine, an Episcopal priest, always says that hope is the most important human emotion, the one that leads to every other positive thing in life. He said that hope is the hand of God on your shoulder. I don't know what the outcome of all this will be, but I didn't feel the hand of God on my shoulder after my conversation with Frank Buchannan. He doesn't think there can be a cure.

After my meeting with Frank Buchannan, I had lunch with Barbara Auletta in a dining room next to her office at FBI Headquarters in Washington. Barbara ate a meatball hero with a side of potato salad and a bowl of pretzels. How she remains so slim is a constant mystery to me.

I told her about our Chechen suspect and my conversation with Buster about taking the guy in for interrogation.

"I've got great news, Barb. Buster found out that Dmitri Pushkin is here illegally. We have the grounds to take him into custody. Bennie Weinberg will supervise the interrogation while the guy is under sodium pentothal."

"You realize, Rick, that you need corroborative evidence to back up an interrogation under sodium pentothal."

"Barb, if Frank Buchannan achieves a breakthrough based on what Pushkin tells us, that's all the corroborative evidence we need. We can put him away for life. But the most important goal is getting scientific evidence. Prosecuting the guy will be secondary."

"Rick, there's something that concerns me. You're close to this case, closer than you should be. I didn't take you off the case after the episode with Ellen, but I almost did. In a meeting, I heard you casually say that you wanted to blow somebody's head off. Your words."

"Barb, there's a growing list of people who want to blow somebody's head off, starting with the President of the United States. Don't worry. I'm working this like a pro, like I always do."

"The difference between you and the president is that you carry a gun. Rick, I trust you. Keep your mind focused on the task, not revenge."

"Barbara, you know me better than that."

Does she?

# CHAPTER FORTY-SIX

The day after my trip to Washington, I went to the New Horizons Nursing Home to visit Ellen. It was a beautiful day, about 75 degrees with a bright sun. Nancy Langdon, Ellen's nurse and my good friend, escorted Ellen to meet me in the open courtyard behind the home. Nancy seemed to take personal pride in making sure that Ellen looked her best. She wore a yellow sundress with a light blue sweater. Instead of slippers, she wore penny loafers.

I sat at a café table as Nancy and Ellen approached. Ellen's face was changing, or was it my imagination? Still pretty, her features were different from what they were just a few weeks ago. It's hard to describe an emotion on a person's face, but Ellen looked confused. That's the only way I can describe it. Confused. The little scar on her cheek that looked like a dimple when she smiles now just looked like a scar.

Nancy made sure that Ellen got plenty of exercise, especially on the treadmill. Nancy also watched Ellen's diet carefully. As a result, she still had a beautiful figure.

Nancy sat Ellen on the chair next to me. I leaned over and kissed her. Just as the last time I visited, she didn't pull her face away from me. She didn't kiss me, but just seemed to ignore me. I love the scent of her skin, so even if my kiss went unanswered, I'd get a whiff of old times. I held her hand and she smiled. She actually smiled, and her dimple appeared. A few weeks ago, she would pull her hand away from me. She wasn't getting better, but she seemed to be adjusting to her new life.

"Aren't the flowers beautiful, honey," I said, pointing to a flower box along the wall.

"My name's Ellen." That hadn't changed. She seemed to want people to get her name right.

"And what's my name?"

"Who are you?"

"I'm Rick."

"I'm Ellen. Nice to see you, Jack. Why are you crying?"

"Oh, it's just allergies. I'm not crying."

I moved my chair closer to her. Her scent, the heat from her body, her beautiful face, all helped to make me feel better.

"You smell nice, Jack."

"I'm wearing Stetson, your favorite cologne. Here, I have something for you."

I handed her a bottle of Chanel No. 5, my favorite perfume. I had cleared this with Nancy, who thought it was a perfectly good idea.

"Can I put a little on your neck?" She didn't resist, and allowed me put a small amount just under her chin.

"I smell nice, like you."

I read somewhere that your olfactory sense is where memory lives. Maybe my cologne and Ellen's Chanel could help bring back some old memories.

She put her head on my shoulder. I thought I'd pass out I was so happy.

"Where's mommy?"

"She's not here, Ellen. Maybe later."

"Dad, please bring mommy here."

"Sure, honey. I will, later."

"My name's Ellen."

She fell asleep with her head still resting on my shoulder. If she wanted to stay that way until midnight, it was fine by me. I saw Nancy standing over in a corner of the courtyard. She smiled and gave me the thumbs up sign.

# CHAPTER FORTY-SEVEN

B uster arranged for a stakeout of 128 Walton Street, *The Syndrome* manufacturing building in Baltimore. For the three FBI agents he assigned, it was a fairly routine operation. The men had a photograph of Pushkin, and it was a simple, if boring, matter of waiting near the building until they saw him. Their orders were to make the arrest outside the building. A raid would come later after we got information from Pushkin. They waited for eight hours with no success. Buster had already arranged for 24-hour video surveillance. Their instructions were to stake the place out and make arrests during daylight. The surveillance cameras could be monitored overnight and they could make the arrest the following day, assuming that Mr. Pushkin showed up.

After a week of round-the-clock stakeout, the team was ordered back to the office.

＝〈¦ ¦〉＝

"Rick, it's Buster. Pushkin never showed up. We've staked out the building for a week and he never appeared. I put him on our watch list when I first learned about him, but he hasn't left the States, not by plane anyway. It's possible that he's just not at the factory, but that doesn't make sense. Here's what I suggest we do. My guys have placed surveillance cameras around the building. We'll keep monitoring the place remotely. If we see Pushkin enter, we'll just stake out the building until he leaves. That's all we can do at this point."

"Buster, did you check with the Baltimore police to see if a body matching his description may have showed up?"

"Rick, do you think I'm an amateur? Of course I checked the police records, and not just Baltimore. I sent his photo to the central database. If something happened to him, we should find out any day."

"Sorry, Buster, I'm just grasping at straws. Where the hell could this guy have gone?"

"And wherever he went, what's he doing there?"

# CHAPTER FORTY-EIGHT

On May 21, the cruise ship *Ocean Ecstasy* left its berth at Port Liberty, New Jersey, and set sail for a week-long cruise to the Caribbean. One of the largest cruise ships afloat, the *Ocean Ecstasy* was 1,100 feet in length. Its 2,700 staterooms could accommodate 6,200 passengers. On this cruise, the ship was almost booked to capacity with 6,166 people aboard, including 1,150 children.

Jack Logan was a 43-year-old FBI agent from the Philadelphia office. He was head of the local narcotics task force, which also brought him into contact with counterterrorism activities. Jack was 5'10" with blond hair and a muscular build. His 42-year-old wife, Bonnie, was 5'7", slim and also blond. Bonnie was a homicide detective with the Philadelphia Police. They hadn't taken a vacation this long in over three years. The Logans had two kids in college, ages 19 and 20. They didn't bring the kids with them on the cruise, looking forward instead to a long romantic date, a date they both agreed had been postponed for too long. Because they were both detectives, they would often joke that they didn't talk, they interrogated one another. Their favorite board game was *Clue.*

Jack and Bonnie stood on the upper promenade deck, sipping their drinks as the ship plied its way out of New York Harbor under the Verrazano Bridge. At 5:20 p.m., the May sun still shone brightly.

After the terrorist attacks on trains and buildings, and the sinking of two cruise ships, security on the *Ocean Ecstasy* was almost military in its precision. Nobody objected to the extra measures, and, in fact, most welcomed them. Seeing armed Coast Guardsmen walking the decks with assault rifles was a new cruise experience for most, but it was something you just got used to. A small platform on the highest deck used to be one of the most popular spots for passengers because of the beautiful views it afforded. But now it was off limits to passengers because the spot was reserved for a sniper.

As two veteran cops—and Agent Jack thought of himself as a cop—they couldn't avoid talking shop, although their goal for the cruise was romance and a rekindling of their love.

"Anything new on *The Syndrome* investigation, Jack?"

"They're keeping it under wraps, hon. Thank God my old friend Rick Bellamy is in charge. With a guy like him on the case, I think they'll eventually crack it. It's the most barbaric goddam terror plot I've ever seen. The idea of spraying young women with a dementia-causing substance is hard to believe. Last report I've heard is that almost 900 women have been hit. I can't believe they even got to my boss, Sarah Watson."

"I hate to feel antsy, Jack, but have you noticed that every time you turn around you see a crew member with a water bottle in his hand?"

"Hey, hon, remember the safety protocol they've been plastering all over TV. If you're sprayed, hold your breath and find water or any kind of liquid and splash down your face. From what I've read, they still don't know what the crap is, but an immediate rinse down seems the only way to fight it. Apparently, the substance is an aerosol, and it only does damage if ingested or breathed in. And another thing: I like the idea that, with all this crazy security, the cruise ship line actually gave us permission to carry our guns. Hell, they even requested it. I don't know about you, but having my Glock on my hip makes me feel better."

"But how will that work with my bikini?"

"I think the idea sounds kind of kinky," he said as he nuzzled Bonnie's neck. "You'll have an interesting tan line."

He pinched her on the butt.

"Hey, Bonnie, we're on vacation. Why don't we stop talking about all this stuff? We're here to relax and not think about the problems of the world. You and I are gonna just be with each other for a change. As far as the problems of the world, fuck it."

"Did you say fuck? That's a wonderful idea."

"Hey, I'm going to give you a spanking for that, potty-mouth lady."

"Spank me? Sounds like fun. Got anything else?"

"I'll think of something. Let's finish these drinks in our stateroom."

⚔

Buster was in my office at 8 a.m. the following morning.

"I've put out a nationwide all-points alert on Pushkin, Rick. It's as if the guy simply disappeared."

"But we don't know what he's up to, Buster. He may not be at the building in Baltimore for a good reason. Maybe he's in a different part of the country working on something else. Hell, maybe he's in bed with the flu. But the photo you had of him was pretty clear. He has a distinctive face. I expect we'll get some kind of lead soon."

Buster's phone sounded.

"Hold it, Rick. This may be something.

"Charles Atkins here."

Buster, the Friendly Spook, often goes by his alias, Charles Atkins.

"It's the Chicago Police Department," he whispered to me as he waited for his caller to get on the line.

"Got it. Right, right. He has his real name on his ID? So you have the guy in custody?

"Looks like you and I are going to Chicago, Rick. They have Dmitri Pushkin in custody, and he matches the photo I sent around. He's even carrying his real ID. We'll take a private CIA jet. I'll round up some assistance and we'll take him to Langley where we can chat."

"Where did they find the guy?" I asked.

"He was about to give a lecture at the Northwestern University psychology department. The subject, according to the online curriculum, was 'Early-Onset Dementia.' I guess he figured nobody would check his immigration status."

"We should take Bennie with us. Bennie can detect bullshit no matter how thick the accent."

⟢⟡⟣

On Sunday, May 22, the *Ocean Ecstasy* cruised off the coast of South Carolina on its way to its first port, St. Thomas, in the Caribbean.

After they ate, Jack and Bonnie Logan went to an upper deck on the outside for an after-dinner drink. The area was large and included two swimming pools and four hot tubs. They took off their robes and climbed into a hot tub. Trying their best to get into vacation mode, they had left their guns in the stateroom safe and their bulletproof vests in the closet. It was 8 p.m. and the sun had set about 20 minutes earlier. It was "formal night," something both Jack and Bonnie hated from their previous cruises. Why waste a relaxing time at sea dressed in formal wear? They both agreed.

About 200 other guests walked, reclined, or swam in the area. The evening was quite warm for late May, about 78 degrees, perfect for relaxing on deck.

They heard a roar coming from inside the ship, not a startling roar, just the sound of hundreds of voices reacting to something. Jack got out of the tub and put on his robe, followed by Bonnie. They were both detectives, so why try to resist the irresistible? They both had to know what just happened.

They walked over to a large window and peered inside. It was a strange, somewhat chaotic scene. People stood and were wringing their hands, flicking off water and wiping their faces and hair with napkins.

"This is the captain speaking. Our deepest apologies, ladies and gentlemen, but we have just suffered an obvious malfunction of the ship's emergency sprinkler system. I've received reports that this happened throughout all interior spaces of the ship, including the bridge. I got a good soaking myself. It was a very fine spray, as you know, and perhaps we should be thankful for that. Thank goodness it only lasted for about 30 seconds. I have assigned additional housekeeping personnel to change the sheets in all staterooms. I feel terrible that your beautiful gowns and handsome tuxedos have been rinsed down. Once again, please accept my apologies. For the remainder of the evening, all drinks are courtesy of the ship."

Jack and Bonnie looked at each other.

"How the hell can an entire sprinkler system just go off?" said Jack. "Aren't those things supposed to be localized to particular areas of the ship?"

"That's my understanding, but I'm no naval engineer. I can't imagine the entire system just opening up."

"Unless somebody planned it," said Jack.

"That would be a pretty stupid practical joke. Why hose down a ship full of people?"

"Maybe it was a disgruntled employee, Bon. Who knows? Hey, we're out on deck having a relaxing time. Why don't we just continue doing exactly that? I think I'll take the captain up on a free drink. You?"

As they stood by the bar, they watched people streaming out onto deck still wiping the water off themselves. Some appeared angry, some laughed, but most seemed to just scratch it off for what the captain said: an accident.

Despite his gentle calming words to the passengers, Captain Magnus Thorssen was furious. A veteran of 25 years with the Royal Caribbean line, Thorssen, a native of Oslo, Norway, was one of the company's most valuable captains. He's known for his charming personality with passengers, but he also has a reputation as a tough, no-nonsense taskmaster with the crew. Raoul Stasi, the ship's engineering officer, stood before the captain on the bridge.

"Raoul, can you give me an explanation for how this happened?"

"Captain, there is only one possibility," said Stasi, with the Portuguese accent of his native Brazil. "This was done on purpose. I have assigned a crew member to watch the valves to make sure it can't be repeated. I have also put a lock on the valves. It's easily broken, as it must be, but it will slow down any joker who tries this again."

"And why was it such a fine spray, almost a fog?"

"Again, sir, I'm convinced that the system was tampered with."

# CHAPTER FORTY-NINE

B ennie, Buster, and I boarded the Gulfstream G600. The CIA knows how to fly in style. Although we didn't discuss it, I figured it was less likely for the jihadis to waste an expensive rocket on a small jet. It still felt uncomfortable to be in the air.

"All the hell we have on this guy is an immigration violation," I said. "It's enough to hold him, but I'm surprised that the Chicago Police Department was so cooperative. They could have looked at it like a simple immigration matter and called the USCIS."

"Rick," said Buster, "don't forget that we have a friend on Pennsylvania Avenue who takes a personal interest in this case. The guy in Chicago mentioned to me that they got a call from the White House."

"How did the White House find out about Pushkin?"

"I called the president's office as soon as I found out that Pushkin was in custody in Chicago."

⊷≺⊹ ⊹≻⊶

The three of us walked into the Chicago Police Headquarters on South Michigan Avenue. The building was large. It was five stories high, and the first floor had no windows, covered instead by amber colored tiles, presumably for security purposes. On the front were the words, "City of Chicago – Public Safety Headquarters." A guard escorted us to Commissioner Daryl Yates' office on the fourth floor.

"I don't know what you people are up to, but I got a call from the White House advising me that my ass was toast if I didn't give you my full cooperation. So, in the interest of keeping my butt at room temperature, I'll do whatever I can to help."

Yates personally walked us to the cell where Pushkin was being held. Pushkin sat alone in his cell, looking subdued. When we entered, he smiled at us. He actually smiled. I had a quick but unfulfilled fantasy of putting a bullet between the bastard's eyes. I was looking at the man who was the reason my Ellen resides at a place called the New Horizons Nursing Home.

I held out my FBI badge and said, "We have some questions for you." I took handcuffs out of my pocket and cuffed him behind his back.

The man spoke perfect English with only a slight accent.

"I can take it from here, fellas," said Commissioner Yates. "You guys go to the back and wait in your car. I'll have two officers bring your prisoner to you. I'm sure you understand that it would raise a lot of questions if my people see three plain clothes taking a prisoner away."

We saw no problem with Yate's idea, so we just went to wait by our car.

"I have to congratulate you, Rick, for a commendable display of professionalism," said Buster.

"What do you mean?"

"Tell me you didn't want to shoot the bastard."

"Yes, I did, I certainly did. But it wouldn't have solved anything by losing our star witness."

As Bennie, Buster, and I chatted, we heard four shots ring out from inside the building. Instinctively, we all pulled out our guns. A uniformed cop came running out the door with his gun pointed high.

"There's been a shooting while a prisoner was being escorted," said the cop. "I think the commissioner was hit. Please stay put here and keep your weapons handy."

A couple of minutes later, a man in a suit appeared at the door. "Please come this way, gentlemen." He motioned us to an office near the rear door of the building.

"I'm Deputy Commissioner McDonald. Commissioner Yates has been shot and killed, along with the prisoner he was escorting."

"Who was the shooter?" Buster and I yelled simultaneously.

"I'm embarrassed to say this," said McDonald "but at this point, we don't know his identity. The guy wore a Chicago Police uniform, but nobody recognized him after the shooting. After he shot the commissioner and the prisoner, he then killed himself. I know you guys are here on some high-level assignment, but please understand that we have some questions for you."

"And *we* have some questions for *you*," I said loudly.

Shit. The most important lead in the entire investigation is now dead. Somebody obviously knew what we were up to. Somebody knew we were interested in Pushkin for more than an immigration violation, somebody who put out a hit and ordered a suicide to keep Pushkin quiet.

"I'm calling my guy at the White House to let him know what happened," said Buster.

After he got off the phone, he looked at Ben and me. "Any thoughts?"

"We've got to raid that place in Baltimore—now!" I said.

# CHAPTER FIFTY

On May 24, Jack and Bonnie Logan had breakfast in one of the main dining rooms. Life on the ship was settling down after the sprinkler incident two days ago, but something seemed wrong, something extremely wrong.

"Jack, is it me or are people acting weird?"

"No, it's not you. I bumped into that nice guy we met yesterday, Phil from Milwaukee. He didn't recognize me. Hell, we must have chatted with him and his wife for an hour yesterday, but it's like he never saw me before. And what about that cute little kid we spoke to? We were amazed that a six-year-old could be so talkative and friendly. I saw him this morning. Not a word out of him. He just stared, not recognizing me at all. Maybe people are having a hard time adjusting to the fresh sea air?"

"Does that explanation satisfy you, Jack?"

"No, it doesn't, hon. I don't know what the hell is going on. Half the people I saw this morning looked like friggin zombies. We met dozens of people while we were boarding. Now they're wandering around like space cadets. Let's take a walk and see what's up."

Jack and Bonnie walked from one group of people to another. The people, including the kids, broke down into two separate groups, those who acted normally and those who seemed to have a far-away stare.

"Good morning, friend," Jack said to one of the ship's officers. They had met the guy yesterday and had a long chat. He was from Philadelphia, and they enjoyed a few minutes of "you must know so and so."

The officer appeared confused. Bonnie noticed that his shirt hung out of his trousers, not a normal sight on an officer aboard a Royal Caribbean ship.

"I don't speak English," said their Philadelphia friend in perfect English. He walked on, without an apparent direction in mind.

They walked up to a Canadian guy they had a brief chat with two days before.

"Peter, if I recall," said Jack as he offered his hand.

"Yes, and you're the FBI guy. Hey Jack, what the hell is going on here? Half the people I meet are zoned out. Do you think something was in the food?"

"Let me ask you a question, Peter," said Bonnie. "When that sprinkler thing happened the other night, were you out on deck?"

"Yes, I was. Do you think the sprinkler may have had something to do with what we're seeing?"

⊫ ⊨

"Mr. and Mrs. Logan, report to the bridge, please," came an announcement over the ship's speakers.

Jack and Bonnie gave each other a "what the hell?" look.

"This is becoming an interesting cruise, Bon. Let's go to the bridge."

"Jack, let's stop by our stateroom and get our guns and vests first."

Jack put on his Kevlar vest with a large "FBI" stenciled on the front and back. Bonnie put on her "Philadelphia Police Department" vest. They both put their guns in holsters on their belts.

When Jack and Bonnie entered the bridge, the first thing Jack noticed was an absolute lack of security. Since 9/11, and especially since 10/15, a ship's bridge was guarded as closely as the cockpit on an airplane. They noticed Captain Thorssen sitting in a chair. He looked at them, smiled, and said, "God morgen." ("Good morning" in Norwegian.)

A young, fit looking man wearing a white officer's uniform strode up to them with his hand extended. He recognized them from the photo database on the computer system. He was an American officer.

"I'm Bill Rugirello, the ship's third mate. My job is basically assistant navigator. Thank you both for coming up to the bridge. I know from Royal Caribbean that you folks are investigators, and that you, Mr. Logan, are an FBI agent. The company keeps track of any law enforcement people on a cruise."

"Please call us Jack and Bonnie, Mr. Rugirello. May we call you Bill?"

"Of course. To crack a stupid joke, I suppose you're wondering why I've gathered you here this morning."

"Yes, we are wondering just that, Bill. But do you mind if I first ask you about the captain. He doesn't look well," Jack said in a soft voice.

"You've heard the captain on the ship's public address system, yes? And you probably remember that his English is almost perfect with only a slight Scandinavian accent. Well here's the story. The captain appears to have forgotten every word of English. Not only that, but he doesn't recognize me. I've noticed that a number of the other officers are acting strangely as well."

"Bill," said Bonnie, "Jack and I feel like we're on the set of an Alfred Hitchcock movie. We've met a lot of people, people we've become friendly with, who now simply don't recognize us. And it started this morning."

"Bill," said Jack, "why don't you give us your take on the situation."

"This may sound crazy, but it's why I asked to see you two. With all the news lately about that crazy disease they call *The Syndrome*, I'm having a suspicion that it may have hit the ship. From what I've read and heard, the disease has only struck young women, and the apparent weapon is a water bottle. It usually takes effect within 48 hours. Remember the sprinkler mess from two days ago? It was a spray, very fine, almost like a fog. Sort of like a gigantic water bottle. I just thank God that I was outside on deck when it happened. I know the FBI is on top of this. Any thoughts?"

"Oh, my God," said Jack. "I need to place a call to New York. Do you have a way for me to do that other than my cell phone? The reception isn't too great."

Rugirello handed him a phone from the console on the bridge.

"This is Agent Logan from the Philadelphia FBI office. I need to speak to Rick Bellamy. It's urgent."

"Hi, Jack, it's Rick. I'm in a car on the way to O'Hare airport in Chicago. My secretary just patched you through. What's up?"

As a trained FBI agent, Jack gave Rick Bellamy a crisp but detailed review of what happened on the *Ocean Ecstasy* in the past two days.

"Jack, I agree. It sounds like *The Syndrome*. The jihadis have apparently expanded their list of targets to include men and children. How many people are aboard?"

"I'm putting you on speaker, Rick, so Bill Rugirello, the ship's third mate, can fill you in."

"Fine, but I'd like to speak to the captain."

"Rick, check your email. I just sent you a photo of the captain. It will explain why you can't talk to him. Besides his physical appearance, you'll be interested to know that in two days he's forgotten the English language. He speaks only Norwegian, when he speaks at all."

"Mr. Bellamy, Bill Rugirello here. In answer to your question, the ship is carrying just shy of 6,200 passengers, and a crew of 1,000. I can't give you exact numbers, but most of the passengers and crew were affected. A few hundred people, including the Logans and myself, were on exterior decks when the sprinklers went off. Bottom line is that we have a few thousand people wandering around like zombies."

"Bill," said Rick Bellamy, "do you know how to drive that thing?"

"Yes, sir. I'm not a captain, but I, along with a few of my fellow officers who weren't affected, can get this thing into port. Besides, I've alerted Royal Caribbean and they're sending another ship to meet us."

"Rick, it's Jack. I won't even ask you because I don't have a need to know, but I hope to hell you guys in counterterrorism are closing in on these bastards. Have you ever seen a cute little kid with obvious signs of dementia? It's not pretty. I hope everything is okay, or at least stable, with your wife, Ellen. Rick, this is one ugly fucking war."

"That it is, my friend. That it is. Jack, as of right now, the *Ocean Ecstasy* is an FBI crime scene, and you're in charge. Wear you're badge and make sure you carry your gun. I'm deputizing Bonnie as a provisional FBI agent. I'll contact the White House, and a helicopter will arrive shortly. I want you both to interrogate any people who haven't been affected by the spray.

"Okay, folks, I've got to call the White House. Please be safe. Jack, you and I will be in touch quite a bit in the next few days. I'm going to give you to my secretary in New York who will take down the contact numbers, including your exact position. I think President Reynolds made an understatement when he called this thing World War III."

# CHAPTER FIFTY-ONE

I turned off my phone after speaking to Jack and Bonnie Logan on the *Ocean Ecstasy*. I had put my phone on speaker so Bennie and Buster could hear the conversation.

"Are you authorized to do what you just did?" asked Buster.

"I don't know, but I just did it."

"You're getting as bad as me."

"I'll take that as a compliment, Buster."

I called Barbara Auletta to let her know about the *Ocean Ecstasy*. I told her she'd be hearing from Jack Logan on the ship.

"So the jihadis have figured out a way to mass produce the shit that causes *The Syndrome*,"

said Bennie. "The scumbags have expanded their market to include men and children."

"Looks like a new front in this fucking war has just opened," I said. "Okay, let's get back to our conversation about Pushkin."

"Here's the way I see it," said Bennie. "They know what we're after, and they knew that Pushkin could have tipped us off. Nobody commits murder and suicide—in a police headquarters of all places —unless the stakes are big."

My cell phone rang. "I gotta take this call, guys."

After I hung up, I looked at Ben and Buster.

"That was McDonald, the Deputy Commissioner in Chicago. They traced the shooter. He comes from Saudi Arabia. He was on the FBI watch list as a known terrorist. How the guy obtained a Chicago PD uniform and simply walked into headquarters is beyond me. It's also beyond the Chicago PD brass. McDonald sounded embarrassed as hell, and he should be. This was an al-Qaeda or ISIS operation; but more important, it tells me they're on to us, big time. What scares me is that we hardly have time to plan a raid. That takes a lot of time and coordination. I can hear that stuff being flushed down toilets in Baltimore now."

"Rick, your lack of faith upsets me. I've been planning a raid ever since we first saw the place in Baltimore. I used my credentials as a deputy FBI Agent. I'm sure you understand. There's an FBI SWAT team with 12 agents on location across the street from 128 Walton Street as we speak. I also arranged for Doctor Frank Buchannan to be there to supervise the gathering of the substances. They should be good to go tomorrow. And that guy you've met before, Lieutenant Leo Burton, who used to be with the Navy SEALs, is in command of the operation."

Bennie and I looked at each other and cracked up. Buster, the Action Figure, was on the case as usual.

"It's great that Burton will be in charge of the attack," I said. "He was the guy in charge of raiding the place where Ellen and the MacPhersons were held hostage. He is one smart and tough hombre.

"Gentlemen," I continued, "this Baltimore raid can't come soon enough."

Lt. Burton addressed his men in a room across the street from 128 Walton Street. His group consisted of 12 highly trained FBI SWAT team officers.

"This operation is going to be tricky because we'll all be wearing bulky hazmat suits. Our objective is to grab any bottle or beaker containing a liquid. As you've been briefed, we think the stuff we're after is the substance that's been causing dementia. We know what the inside of 128 Walton looks like, and we even have a live video feed."

Two nights before, Burton had one of his men drill a hole in the skylight and drop a surveillance video camera into the building. He flashed the camera feed onto a monitor.

"As you can see, there are two long tables that appear to be for assembly of some sort. Over there toward the right appears to be a tank. Doctor Buchannan, do you have any thoughts or questions?"

"Well, first I have to tell you guys something," said Buchannan. "That call I just got was from Rick Bellamy at 26 Federal Plaza. I'll summarize. The enemy has figured out how to produce the substance in huge quantities. They probably did it right here in the building you're about to raid. They attacked a cruise ship, spreading the substance with the ship's sprinkler system. That was two days ago. Now thousands of people, including men and children, have come down with *The Syndrome.* You guys are about to launch the most important attack since Jimmy Doolittle's raid over Tokyo in 1942. Now to get back to Lieutenant Burton's question about my thoughts. We have two objectives, Lieutenant. We want to grab every piece of paper you can lay your hands on, and collect as much of the substance as possible. That means you guys will have to be careful if shooting starts. We don't want to waste any of the substance."

"You mean *when* the shooting starts, Doctor. This is going to be a firefight. I've gone over lines of sight with my guys here, and we know we have to try to keep the bullets away from any equipment."

"I've heard that you guys are tough," said Buchannan. "Now I'm seeing it with my own eyes. We don't know how long the substance remains viable in the atmosphere, so make sure you have your hazmat suits zipped tight. Another thing: Please take as many prisoners alive as you can for interrogation. Is that possible?"

"Doc, we think of ourselves as the '72 Virgins Dating Service,' but we'll do what we can. If any man has a gun or is wearing one on a holster, we'll engage him."

"Engage?"

"Yes, we'll kill him."

"And they say that scientists talk funny," said Buchannan.

"See that man in the white lab coat, Lieutenant?" said Buchannan pointing to the monitor. "He's holding a clipboard. If at all possible, we'd like to take him alive."

"Again, Doc, we'll do what we can. From our days of surveillance, we know that a lot of these men leave the building at night. Usually, only four or five remain behind, including the lab coat guy. We have FBI agents stationed all around this building. When one of these pricks takes off for the evening, he'll be stopped on the street."

"What time will the raid begin, Lieutenant?"

"Two a.m., Doctor. We do our best work at the wee hours. Have you arranged for the hazmat truck from CDC?"

"Yes, it's parked around the corner."

"Anything else you can think of, Doc?"

"Yes, remember to grab any piece of paper and take it with you. Don't forget to check file cabinets."

At 2:00 a.m. on May 25, two SWAT team sharpshooters aimed their rifles at the security cameras that lined the roof of 128 Walton Street. Within 20 seconds, all the cameras were blind. As they had

counted, four men left the building by nightfall, leaving five behind. All of the agents were dressed in hazmat suits. On command, two agents broke down the door with a battering ram. The interior consisted of one large room and two smaller office spaces. The agents already knew this from the interior surveillance camera. Two men rushed to the offices, kicked in the doors and opened fire. Agent Arnold Groner tackled and handcuffed a tall man in a lab coat.

Two other agents shot two men who stood by a table in the large room. The planning for the raid included careful line of fire coordination to avoid shooting any bottles or beakers that may contain the substance. Within three minutes, four enemy personnel were dead and one was in custody. According to instructions, two of the agents packed up every file folder and piece of paper they could find.

Frank Buchannan walked up to the table that was covered with glass beakers and spray bottles.

"Great shooting, men. Not one of the pieces of evidence was hit."

A medium-sized hazmat truck pulled up to the rear of the building. Buchannan supervised the removal of all materials from the factory. The truck, escorted by four police cars with sirens blaring, proceeded on its way to the nearest Centers for Disease Control facility in Washington. The main headquarters was in Atlanta, but Buchannan thought it was too far to travel with the substance, especially since he had no idea about its shelf life.

The Baltimore raid was a success.

⟩⟨

Bennie, Buster, and I fidgeted in our seats in my office. We had been told that the Baltimore raid would go down at 2 a.m., and we wanted to be ready to receive a briefing. Our stomachs were in a collective knot.

Buster's phone rang.

"Got it. Great. Fucking outstanding. You deserve the Medal of Freedom, Frank. Let's talk soon, real soon."

From what we heard, Buster didn't have to tell us that it was Dr. Frank Buchannan with good news.

"Four of the bad guys are dead, and three in custody, including two who left the building earlier. One of the men they arrested was wearing a lab coat, and Buchannan thinks he may be a technician or maybe even a scientist. Not a drop of substance has been spilled. It's on its way to the CDC facility in Washington."

"That's the good news," I said, "but without Pushkin to talk to, we just have to hope he left some document with formulas on it so Frank and his medical snoops can figure it out."

"Hey, Rick," said Buster. "Remember that your wonderful wife put you on a regimen of positive thinking. Let's take the good news as it comes. I don't know about you, but I'm going to have a Scotch on the rocks. And while we're at it, how about a couple of Jerry Seinfeld jokes."

"I could use both the Scotch and the Seinfeld jokes," said Bennie. "It's too late to go to bed."

# CHAPTER FIFTY-TWO

O n May 30, five days after the Baltimore raid, my alarm went off as usual at 5:30 a.m. I actually slept through the night. When I first awoke, I couldn't figure out why I was in the guest room. Then reality dawned on me, as it does every morning. I was alone.

Following Ellen's plan to help my stress, I did 20 minutes of yoga, followed by a 20-minute meditation. I poured myself a cup of coffee, my *one* cup of regular coffee for the day. I had Ellen's plan taped to the wall in the breakfast nook. I couldn't make myself cross out step number one of the plan, "sex with Ellen." Imagining that it may happen someday helped keep my sanity.

I was having a bowl of cereal with sliced banana when the phone rang at 7:15.

"Good morning, Rick, it's Bill Reynolds."

Bill Reynolds? Bill Reynolds? I know that name from somewhere.

Holy shit, it's the President of the United States.

"Good morning, Mr. President."

"Rick, I have a favor to ask. Could you come to Washington today? I'll meet you at Walter Reed Hospital. I want you to see Amanda."

"Of course, sir. I'll make arrangements right now."

"The travel arrangements have already been made, Rick. A car will pick you up at 9:30. See you later."

"Yes, sir."

President Reynolds wants me to meet the First Lady, the poor stricken First Lady. But why?

I called Buster and Barbara. They both asked why I was going to Washington and I told them.

"You don't get a call from the president unless it's something important, Rick," said Barbara. "Please call me when you can."

"My spook's sixth sense tells me that Reynolds has more in mind than a social visit to a woman with dementia," said Buster.

I had no idea what the day was about to bring.

———※ ※———

I walked into Walter Reed Hospital at 12:30 p.m. A White House staffer named Marilyn was in the lobby to greet me, along with a Marine sergeant. We took the elevator to the fourth floor, where the First Lady's room was located. It was not a typical hospital floor. Armed Marines and assorted other personnel milled about. Marilyn, the staffer, led me to Amanda Reynolds' room, where the president was waiting. Amanda was sitting in a chair in the corner of the private room.

"Honey, this is my good friend Rick Bellamy who I told you about," the president said.

Amanda smiled, stood, and extended her hand. "Nice to meet you, Rick. Thank you for coming to visit me. Would you like a cup of coffee?"

"No, thank you, ma'am."

"President Bill has told me all about you. He also told me about your lovely wife, Ellen. How is she doing?"

The thought crossed my mind how embarrassing it would be if my head exploded all over the room. This woman didn't appear to be suffering from anything. She has *The Syndrome*? I saw her "speech" at the Waldorf. I actually watched her coming down with the disease, her confused look, her fumbling for words. What the hell is going on? I decided to engage Amanda in a full-blown conversation, not the stilted one-liners people use when communicating with a dementia patient.

"Ellen is doing as well as can be expected. I see her every day. The home is only a few blocks from our apartment. I'm sure she'd love to meet you."

"And I'd love to meet her. She's quite a woman. A world-class architect who knows how to handle an AK-47. I've read all about her in the papers. When did she come down with this thing everybody is calling *The Syndrome*?"

"On April 4, Mrs. Reynolds. It happened overnight."

"I hear you, Rick. That shit hits you like a ton of bricks. And please call me Amanda."

Okay screw it. That's it. Something is out of focus here. I'm having a conversation with a woman who is supposed to be in advanced dementia, but she seems totally normal. I'm going to find out what the hell is going on.

"Mrs. Reynolds, Amanda, if you don't mind me saying, you seem to be in perfect health."

"Other than a bit of a headache, I'm feeling just fine, Rick, and thank you for noticing. Bill told me that you were on hand for my command performance at the Waldorf. People tell me I was quite a hit. Apparently, I kept calling Hugh Jackson 'Jimmy,' and asking him what the fuck everybody was doing there." She cracked up laughing.

"Yes, I was there, Amanda. It broke my heart, along with a lot of other hearts in the room. But if you have *The Syndrome*, how can we be having this conversation. I don't get it."

"I think I'll let POTUS over here explain it to you."

President Reynolds was grinning like a happy Golden Retriever.

"Rick, I wanted you to be the first to see this. When Amanda checked in here, she looked like the *Night of the Living Dead.*"

"Thanks for the compliment, Prince Charming," she said as she reached over and grabbed his hand.

"I've invited a guy who I think you want to talk to," said the president. "He can explain everything."

Dr. Frank Buchannan walked into the room, smiling as if he was rehearsing for a toothpaste commercial. The good doctor, normally a shy intellectual kind of guy, walked up to me and gave me a bear hug.

"The last time I saw you, Rick, I said that I was cautiously optimistic that we may have been on the road to a discovery, a vaccine. The raid on that place in Baltimore nailed it for us. Even though the jihadis disposed of Dmitri Pushkin, that evil bastard, we found the documents we needed. It became a process of reverse engineering. We discovered exactly what the substance was, and, working from there, we looked to find something that could reverse the symptoms. Yes, you heard me—reverse the symptoms. Rick, we found a cure—a fucking cure, not just a vaccine. It was amazingly simple. Remember when I told you about my hunch that we may be looking at a bacteria?"

"Remember?" I said. "It was the only good news I had heard in weeks. So you're telling me that your hunch paid off?"

"Big time, Rick. We found that the substance was a combination of various bacteria, mixed in a brilliantly evil way by Pushkin. I then formed a hunch that we may have an already existing antibiotic that could act on *The Syndrome*. It's Tralforlalazine, an effective but seldom used drug for treating the flu. The great thing about it was that it had been widely tested in clinical trials and approved by the FDA five years ago. We already knew its side effects, which are rare and relatively mild—joint pain and headaches—both of which can be helped with over-the-counter medications like ibuprofen. When I told the president about it, and how it was relatively risk free, he insisted that we administer it to the First Lady. Within 12 hours, she was symptom-free. And this happened with the first dose of the medication. I've prescribed a seven-day regimen. We'll see where it goes from there. It's possible that none of the people affected will ever have to take another dose. We have our fingers crossed with the children who got infected on the *Ocean Ecstasy*, but, so far, the results are excellent. You see Mrs. Reynolds here with your own eyes. Yes, we didn't just find a vaccine, we found the cure," he said as he grabbed my shoulders and stared into my eyes.

"Frank, you know what my next question is."

"Yes, I do, Rick. You want to know when we can give the drug to your wife, Ellen. Well, because the drug is a simple prescription medication, we didn't need to get your permission as next of kin."

"So what are you telling me, Frank? Did you give her the fucking stuff or not?"

"Why don't you turn around, Rick?"

Sometimes events go by so fast your mind doesn't come up with words. But when Frank told me to turn around, I thought of one word, a word I'd almost forgotten—hope. I remembered my Episcopal priest friend and his words to me about the meaning of the word hope. I felt the hand of God on my shoulder.

"Hi, honey. How about a kiss?" Ellen said as she walked into the room, wearing a beautiful yellow dress and a healthy dose of Chanel No. 5.

My FBI Agent tough-guy pose abandoned me. I bawled like an infant as Ellen and I hugged. I thought back over the weeks to April 4, the worst day of my life. But suddenly I found myself savoring the happiest moment of my life. It was one of those peak-of-life experiences that will never leave me. My Ellen was back.

"So, what's new, Rick?" Ellen asked. She has always had an amazing way of finding just the right touch of humor at the right time. My tears turned to laughter. Everybody else in the room laughed too, especially Amanda Reynolds, who totally cracked up.

"Oh, nothing much," I said, feeding the good humor of the moment. "What's new with you?" I said, wiping my tears away. My mind swam with my new reality.

"Here's one thing that's new. I decided to try something I had always wanted to do, so I picked up a *Time-Life* book at the airport." Ellen then recited the presidents and vice-presidents of the United States from memory, barely pausing for breath. "It only took me five minutes to memorize the list."

"Go, girl!" shouted Amanda.

"Mr. and Mrs. Bellamy" said a White House staffer. Maybe you folks would like to have a little privacy. The president will be holding a press conference in 45 minutes. He asks if you can be part of it, Mrs. Bellamy. That's totally up to you." He escorted us into an adjacent room. These White House types are classy operators, I thought.

I've never fainted in my life. It's just something that never happened to me. But I felt close. After weeks of despair, weeks of returning to an empty apartment, weeks without hope, there was Ellen, *my Ellen,* standing there in front of me, totally alert.

"Hon, the past few weeks have been the worst in my life, worse even than the time you were kidnapped. You couldn't even remember my name. You thought I was your father. Does your nurse, Nancy, know about this? She and I have become good friends recently."

"Yes, she does. We had breakfast this morning before I caught my flight. Here's a selfie she took and asked me to show you."

There was Nancy, grinning broadly and flashing the thumbs up sign with her free hand.

"Have you been following my plan for the new Rick?"

"Yes, every day, except of course for number one. You remember what number one is?"

"Do I ever. We're going to work on that with extreme diligence when we get home. Got any good Seinfeld jokes for me?"

"I will as soon as my phone rings."

# CHAPTER FIFTY-THREE

We were still in our private room. I was slowly adjusting to the life that flowed into me. I couldn't let go of Ellen, even if I wanted to, and I didn't.

"Rick, tell me everything about the past few weeks. Nurse Nancy said I should hear it from you. I feel like I'm missing part of my life. Well, I guess I am. The last thing I recall was having lunch with you after a meeting at your office. I have a vague recollection that something upsetting happened. So talk to me, hon, where have I been?"

"Yes, it started with lunch at Chez Amis. You went to get cash from the ATM machine and came back to the table really upset. You had forgotten your bank PIN number, one that you used for years."

"You mean 435927?"

"If that's what you say it is, I know it's the number."

We kissed again.

"When I got home that night, I realized that something terrible was going on. Instead of greeting me at the door like you always did, you sat in the den and stared at a blank TV screen. Every time I called you 'hon' or 'honey,' you said that your name was Ellen. I called Bennie to come over the next day. That clinched it. We were both convinced that you had some kind of crazy fast onset Alzheimer's disease. You didn't remember Bennie at all. I hired a wonderful private duty nurse named Olga on Bennie's suggestion. No way would I leave you alone. When I came home that first day, Olga was upset that you had gotten worse in a single day. I knew I had to get you into a full-time facility. That was also Bennie's suggestion."

"What was I like at the nursing home, the place called New Horizons?"

"Like a zombie, to be blunt. I visited you every day. You kept confusing me with your father. After a while, your agitation stopped, your coldness changed, and you actually showed some affection—for your father. It seemed that you were adjusting to your new reality."

"You mean my lack of reality?"

"Yeah, I guess that's more accurate. But let me ask you a question, babe. Is it okay if I call you babe or do you insist on Ellen?"

"Babe, honey, sweetheart, Ellen—call me whatever you want. Just keep telling me you love me."

"I love you. But getting back to my question. Frank said he gave you the medication less than 12 hours ago. What was it like coming back to the real world?"

"The best way I can describe it is waking up from a long sleep. Nothing dramatic, just a sudden realization that I didn't know where I was or why I was there. I talked to Amanda Reynolds about this and she had the same experience."

"So what about this press conference? Do you think you can handle it?"

"Yeah, I think it's important. I think I have an obligation to let all the other people who were hit with this shit know how I'm feeling. From what I've been told, until just over a week ago, only young women were attacked. Then came that horrible sprinkler event on that cruise ship. My God, almost 6,000 people were hit with this *Syndrome* thing. But at the news conference, I'll just answer questions. I don't want to upstage the president or Amanda."

"You could upstage the pope if you wanted to. You'll do just fine."

A large room at Walter Reed Hospital was often used for press conferences and announcements. Because Walter Reed is the place where important government officials are hospitalized, it sees its share of journalists.

"Ladies and gentlemen, the President of the United States."

"Good afternoon, my fellow Americans. Today is a day of relief. And speaking for myself, I can also say that it's a day of joy. In the past few weeks, as you know, over 900 American women were struck down with a terrible illness, an illness that we first thought was a fast-acting form of early-onset Alzheimer's disease. And then, just shy of a week ago, the cruise ship *Ocean Ecstasy* saw almost 6,000 men, women, and children come down with the symptoms. We now know that the illness wasn't natural. It was the result of a weaponized substance delivered with a spray bottle, or, in the case of the cruise ship, sent through a sprinkler system. The result was an affliction that we've called *The Syndrome*. We've learned that our enemy called it The Scent of Revenge.

"Because of the diligent efforts of countless people, we found the solution, the cure. Special thanks goes to the brilliant physician, Doctor Frank Buchannan, who isolated the substance and discovered a simple cure, a prescription medication that already exists. Because our policy is not to divulge the names of government agents who were involved in clandestine operations, I just say thank you. You know who you are. But I can single out one agent, because his own wife was a victim, and he played a crucial role in enabling Doctor Buchannan to find the cure. Let's hear it for FBI Agent Rick Bellamy."

I only wished that Buster, Bennie, and Barbara Auletta could be there with me.

"Next to me is my wonderful wife, the First Lady, Amanda Reynolds. Amanda came down with *The Syndrome* a few weeks ago as she was giving a speech in New York City. We'll never forget the horror of watching her, one of the most articulate women in America, as she stumbled for words. I'm now going to ask Amanda to speak. She's much better at it than I am, so I'm sure you'll all be pleased."

The room thundered with applause for Amanda Reynolds.

"Thanks, Bill, or am I supposed to call you Mr. President?" Good laugh line.

"I'm happy that my new found friend, Ellen Bellamy, is here with us this afternoon, a woman who shares with me the strange sisterhood of the past few weeks. I'm going to ask Ellen to stand next to me, and we can both share our experience with you. Ellen, do you have any recollection of the last thing that happened to you before you drifted into dementia?"

"Yes, Mrs. Reynolds—"

"The name's Amanda, my friend."

"Yes, Amanda. I was having lunch with my husband, Rick. I went to an ATM to get some cash, and realized that I forgot my PIN number. I just recall being upset, because normally I have a photographic memory."

"Do you remember it now, hon?"

"I'm happy to announce 435927! It's no longer valid, but I just love to say it—because I can remember it. If there's a horse with that number, I think I'll play it."

The crowd roared with laughter. The First Lady had nothing on Ellen.

"And my experience after I was given the medication, as you and I have compared notes, Amanda, was like waking up after a long sleep."

"Ellen, this won't take a long time because you do it so fast, but would please share with the American people the little memory game you learned on the plane coming here? I believe you said it took you five minutes to memorize the list."

With that, Ellen recited the names of every American president and vice-president starting with George Washington. The crowd stomped and cheered. Some people, like me, cried.

"Ladies and gentlemen, let's hear it for my new best girlfriend."

More cheers. This was the most unreal press conference I'd ever attended.

"The great news, and yes, we'll answer your questions in a moment, but the truly great news is that all of the 900 women who've been afflicted with *The Syndrome* have been given the medication. A small army of doctors and nurses are now delivering the medication to the people afflicted on the *Ocean Ecstasy*. Our lost fellow citizens are coming back to us. People like Maria Adams, Deputy Secretary of State; Angela Johnston, President of the University of Michigan; Regina Townsend, CEO of the New York Stock Exchange; Joan Paddington, CEO of Megasoft; Georgina Laughlin, Secretary of Commerce; Mary Escobedo, CEO of Suresoft; Jane Lopez, Secretary of the Interior; Florence Lambda, Deputy Secretary of Defense; Dolores Estrada, Senior Director, NASA; Aimee Pierce, CEO of United Way; and Rear Admiral Ashley Patterson. I don't have time to name them all, but I'm delighted to say that all of these wonderful Americans are now back with us."

# CHAPTER FIFTY-FOUR

Ellen and I sat in a restaurant at the airport waiting for our flight back to New York.

"Rick, I think I have a great idea for that gigantic bonus that Angus MacPherson gave me."

"Eighteen million, I remember it well. Didn't you say you were thinking of setting up a foundation to help kids?"

"I have a better idea. What I just went through, along with those other people, had a happy ending, thank God. But what about the millions of people who have the real Alzheimer's, real dementia? Frank Buchannan found a cure for *The Syndrome* in no time. He was able to find it because he knew the cause—the substance in the spray bottles. So the other women and I suffered from the symptoms of Alzheimer's, but, as we know, it wasn't Alzheimer's. I want to start a foundation to fund research on the real Alzheimer's disease. With my big bonus, we can provide a lot of seed money. Since the other victims and I have gotten so much press, it should be easy to shake the money trees. Because his daughter Jane was a victim, I'm sure Mr. Money Bags, Angus MacPherson, would love to make a big contribution.

"Rick, I was out of commission for almost two months. People with Alzheimer's have no hope, and neither do their families. Imagine yourself visiting me for the rest of my life at the New Horizons Nursing Home. I want to find a cure, or at least a treatment, for Alzheimer's, and other forms of dementia. And part of the mission will be support for the families of the victims. Everybody calls me and the other women the victims. But I don't remember what happened, and the others don't either. I didn't suffer. It's like I was just asleep. You, Rick, and the other family members were the real victims. You were the ones who suffered. I want to support those people. Do you like my idea?"

How typical of Ellen. She just came back to the world after weeks in a mental wilderness, and what does she think about? Helping other people. That's Ellen.

"Yes, I like your idea. And I *love* you."

Ellen and I walked into our apartment at 5:50. I grabbed her by the shoulders. "Do you have any idea what it was like coming home without you here?"

"That's history, Rick. I'm here now, and I'll always be here for you."

We walked into the den. When I turned on the light, a bunch of people shouted, "Surprise!"

There was Bennie; Buster; Barbara Auletta; Olga Burns, the private duty nurse; and Nancy Langdon, Ellen's nurse from New Horizons.

"We had to do this, guys," said Buster. "We know you two have some catching up to do, but we had to see you."

Buster, who has a key to our apartment, had arranged for a buffet and drinks. He's the classiest spook I've ever met.

Bennie walked up to Ellen and hugged her. "Don't call me Lennie and don't call me George. Ellen, I can't tell you how happy I am." With that, the tough NYPD detective began to cry.

"We all saw the press conference on TV," said Buster. "I didn't think anybody could outshine the First Lady, but you did."

Nancy walked up to Ellen, hugged her, and gave her a package.

"Nancy, you're too kind. I don't remember ever meeting you until I came out of it yesterday, but Rick told me that you were my new mother for a few weeks."

Ellen opened the package. It was a DVD set of *Barney and Friends* reruns. Ellen looked puzzled.

"That was your favorite show," said Nancy.

Ellen laughed and said, "I'll cherish this forever."

Great, I thought. We can binge-watch the purple piece of crap.

The party was great, a welcome home to a person nobody ever thought would come home.

At 7:30 p.m., Buster said, "Folks, I think it's time we leave these two to catch up. Ellen, you're the best thing that ever happened to my friend Rick."

Everybody raised their glasses. Then something happened that I never expected to see, something that put an emotional exclamation point on this perfect day. Buster, Mr. Tough Guy, the fearless spook, broke down in tears.

After everyone left, I took Ellen by the hand and led her to the couch, facing the TV.

"Right where we're sitting was when I realized there was a problem," I said. "When I came home that night, you were sitting here staring at the blank TV. When I stroked your leg, you placed my hand on the couch between us. I went to kiss you and you pulled away." After I said that, she leaned over and kissed me. A long, slow, wet kiss.

"If you don't mind," I said, "I want to turn on the TV. The thought of you staring at a blank screen freaks me out."

"Hey, Mr. Romantic, I want to talk."

"I'll put it on mute." I clicked on the TV.

Ellen got up and walked over to the table where Nancy's gift lay.

"We're going to watch *Barney and Friends*. I want to see what I found so fascinating all those weeks."

We watched Barney for about 10 minutes, chuckling at the lunacy on the screen. Every now and then, Ellen looked at me with a "what the fuck?" expression on her face.

"Rick, are you telling me I actually enjoyed this shit?"

"Your cultural tastes have improved recently, hon."

"I'm going to take a shower," Ellen said. "I feel grungy after a day of travelling."

"Isn't it wonderful that you don't need help bathing?" I said.

"I may not need help, but that doesn't mean I don't want it," she said with a wink.

# CHAPTER FIFTY-FIVE

"Greetings, Brother Gamal. May Allah be with you."

"Bob, I am not Brother Gamal or Gamal Pashez. I am Howard Orlando, and you are Bob McLaughlin."

"I'm sorry, Howard. You're absolutely correct. We must stay in the shadows."

"Bob, The Committee and I have reviewed your photographs of the American electric grid. We all agree that you're a gifted photographer, and your research is also impeccable. Out of the 55,000 substations, you have narrowed the country's electric grid down to nine key locations, nine critical substations. Your notes about the surrounding terrain are invaluable. You're also quite skilled in the use of small drone aircraft. But I do have an important question. Did anyone see you, and more directly, did anyone take *your* picture as you were taking yours?"

"Of course I can't be certain, Howard. I intentionally placed myself at a distance from the power stations to avoid suspicion of any kind. But these were public areas. I have no idea if someone photographed me."

"So you are satisfied that you weren't observed?"

"Yes, sir. If I may add, the locations I photographed are far from secure. If I could fly my drone so close to them, I'm sure they can be taken out."

"Why do you make that observation, Bob?"

"Well, I think it's obvious that we want to target these stations and attack them. I think using drones for attack as well as surveillance is the perfect solution."

"But nobody has discussed any such plan with you, have they? These matters are for The Committee."

"I'm sorry if I overstepped myself, Howard. I was just making an observation."

"Bob, we all must do our jobs, and nothing more. Your job does not require making observations."

"Yes, sir."

"Our meeting has come to a conclusion, Bob. Thank you for coming to visit me."

As McLaughlin walked to the door, Orlando reached into his sports coat and withdrew a pistol. He fired twice at McLaughlin, hitting him square in the back and killing him instantly.

# CHAPTER FIFTY-SIX

"I mam Mike wants to see us, Rick," said Buster. "Same place as usual, the Bethesda Terrace restaurant. We'll see him there at 2 p.m. this afternoon."

Buster and I asked the waitress to sit us at a table near the edge of the outdoor dining area.

"I can't wait to see Mike's outfit. He's become a one-man costume drama," I said.

A private security guard in uniform walked toward us. He had a handlebar mustache and wore dark wraparound sunglasses. It was Mike.

"Good to see you guys. Rick, I can't tell you how happy I am that your wife is okay. Here's a little something for her. I recall you telling me that these are her favorites." He handed me a box of Perugina chocolates.

"Thanks, Mike. I should be giving *you* a gift. Your tip to us about the spray bottles was the key part to the puzzle. I just wish we could thank you publicly."

"Well, I do have a little gift," said Buster. "Mike, you've been invaluable to us in so many matters I can't count them. I've discussed what I'm about to tell you with CIA headquarters. We're putting you on the payroll for $95,000 a year, which isn't bad for part-time work. Here is some fake ID so you can set up a new bank account. The money will be wired weekly to that account."

"Hey, do you think I'm doing this for money?"

"Of course not," said Buster. "You never even hinted that you wanted anything in exchange for your information. But the time you spend on helping us could be spent in other ways. Besides, I get paid, Rick gets paid, and even though you're not full time, you damn well should get paid. Hey, you've got kids in college."

"Thanks, Buster, you flatter me. But I refuse. If you set up an account, I'll refuse to sign the papers. If you send me checks, I'll throw them away. I have a simple goal in life, and it's to stop radical Islam. And I refuse to take money. But thanks anyway. What I want to talk to you about is *The Syndrome*."

"Well, thank God, and thanks in large part to you," I said, "we don't have to worry about that anymore. Every one of the people who were attacked with the substance has been cured, including the passengers on that cruise ship. Do you think it's still something we should be worried about?"

"Let me put it this way, guys. The scumbags in charge of that operation are furious. I've been hearing this all over the place. Those evil pricks actually took joy in destroying the lives of people with that shit they call The Scent of Revenge. It was one of their crowning achievements as they saw it. That place in Baltimore you guys took out was the key to ramping up the campaign. I cannot fucking believe that I share, or shared, a religion with those animals. But mark my word, guys, they're looking for payback. The Super Bowl wasn't enough. Rick, I know that you and your wife came close to being killed in that one. Even the Scent of Revenge wasn't enough. They've got some even bigger stuff planned. They're looking to pull off something big. Oh, yeah, the top dogs at al-Qaeda and ISIS now have a name for the group. They call themselves The Committee."

"Mike, do you have any idea what they're planning?"

"No, Rick. But it's going to be something big."

"Anything else, my friend?" said Buster.

"Yes. I have a study assignment for you guys. I've been reading a lot recently about Ayaan Hirsi Ali, the expatriate from Somalia who became a member of the Dutch Parliament and is now on a jihadi assassination list. I've read all of her books, and now I'm reading her latest. It's entitled *Heretic: Why Islam Needs a Reformation Now*. Guys, I feel like I'm looking into my own mind when I read this brave lady's stuff.

"She says there are three types of Muslims: The Mecca Muslims, the vast majority of the 1.6 billion Muslims in the world. These are devout people, but people who don't want to have anything to do with assimilating into a culture not their own. They prefer to cocoon themselves from society at large. They have a lot of tension with modernity.

"Then there are The Medina Muslims, the radicals. She puts their number at about 48 million. That's a shit load of people. She calls them Medina Muslims because the prophet Muhammad took on a political and military stance when he went from Mecca to Medina. That's when he started to insist that you're either a Muslim or you're an outcast with no rights.

"The third type of Muslims are the Dissident Muslims, a small group of reformers. She considers herself one of them, and so do I. Like me, Ali jumped ship. She thinks that military and political resistance to radical Islam is not the answer, but only a necessary blocking action.

"Ali says the only true hope is a Muslim Reformation, and she came up with five areas that need to change. First, she attacks the faith in Muhammad's semi-divine status, the unquestioned belief in his infallibility, and that the Quran is the literal word of God. Second, she questions the supremacy of the after-life over living in the present. Third, she questions the violent and intolerant parts of Sharia Law. Fourth, she insists on the right of individuals to enforce Islamic law over themselves, rather than by a religious vigilante police force. And fifth, she takes on the whole idea of waging jihad. She says Islam will never be a religion of peace if its followers insist on violent struggle. I'd love to see her quoted about The Scent of Revenge, the kind of evil cruelty that makes her crazy.

"You guys need to read this book, as well as her other books. It will help you to understand all of the shit that's going down. I know it's helped me."

"Mike," I said, "you don't need to convince me. I've read a lot about Ayaan Hirsi Ali, but I haven't read her books. I'm going to do exactly that. But I have a concern, my friend. You need to keep in the background. Please don't promote this brave woman from your pulpit or you'll become a target just like her."

"Don't worry, Rick. I like my head just where it's always been, attached to the rest of my body."

# CHAPTER FIFTY-SEVEN

President Reynolds reinstated Sarah Watson as FBI Director. I've never seen Barbara Auletta, her short-term successor, so relieved. Reynolds had made it clear that Barbara's appointment was interim, so she wasn't embarrassed. We were both totally okay with the way it played out. We both like and respect Sarah Watson, and now that she's back among the living, we were happy to go back to the status quo before *The Syndrome*.

———

"Rick, we're going to have a special visitor today, Sarah Watson. Please round up Buster and Bennie. She wants to see them too."

"Great," I said. "She's been on the phone with Ellen a few times and I've chatted with her, but it will be good to see her."

"Speaking of Ellen, how is she doing?"

"Well, we've started playing chess again. Last night, she checkmated me in seven moves."

"As I recall, Rick, you were a champion chess player in college."

"That doesn't stop her from kicking my ass, Barb. I actually think her memory has gotten better since *The Syndrome*."

⟨⟩

Sarah Watson walked into Barbara's office with her usual flair.

"How the hell are you guys?"

She gave each of us a hug.

Bennie handed her a package. She opened it and saw it was a book entitled *How to Improve Your Memory* by Dr. Benjamin Weinberg.

"Thanks, wise-ass," she said, laughing.

"Do you promise not to throw us out of my office, Sarah?"

"What?"

Barbara told Sarah about the incident when she came down with *The Syndrome*, and how she yelled at us and threw us out of Barbara's office, which she thought was hers.

"Holy shit! It's a blessing that I can't remember anything about my days with *The Syndrome*. So yes, I promise not to throw you guys out of Barbara's office—unless it's necessary." We all laughed.

"So let me bring you folks up to date on a few things, even though I'm the one who's had a lot to catch up on after my unintended vacation. First, you can forget the rumors about President Reynolds declaring martial law. Cooler heads prevailed, including mine. Yes, the right of *habeas corpus* is alive and well in America. The next thing is this: The President wants to assemble all of us women afflicted by *The Syndrome* to convene at a big public meeting in Washington. He thinks it will be a sort of catharsis for the country."

"What do *you* think about that idea, Sarah?" said Barbara.

"I have some definite ideas on the subject, but I want to hear your thoughts."

"May I be blunt, Madam Director?" said Buster.

"Of course, and call me Sarah."

"Sarah, that's the dumbest goddam idea I've heard in a long time. Rick and I met with our inside guy, that imam from Brooklyn. He told us that al-Qaeda is furious about our having found the cure for *The Syndrome*. They considered it their major operation and were looking to expand it from the Baltimore plant, as you know. They got pretty far with that cruise ship attack. The imam said that the top guys freaked out over the cure, and that they're planning something, something big. If we assembled all 900 of the afflicted women in one place, I'd want to see it surrounded by a Marine battalion and circled by Apache helicopters. It would be the most tempting target they could ever want. They could brag that they got beaten once by the cure for *The Syndrome*, and then they killed all of the original victims. And what about the thousands of people, including men and children, who were hit on the *Ocean Ecstasy?*"

"Another thing to consider," said Barbara, "is that *60 Minutes* is planning an entire program about the illness and the cure. They'll send sound crews to interview people all across the country, not assembled in one place as a tempting target, as Buster pointed out."

"I don't think Ellen would do it," I said. "Like you, Sarah, she's living her life again. I doubt she'd want to risk it, no matter how well-intentioned the PR event would be. Besides, I'll tie her to a chair and bolt the door."

"Well," said Watson, "you folks pretty much sum up my thoughts on the subject. The *60 Minutes* people will do their usual excellent work, and a lot of women won't be put at risk. The producer has already been in touch with me. How about Ellen, Rick?"

"Yes, they've been in contact with us. They want me and a bunch of other husbands to be on the segment as well. I don't think that part is a good idea. As head of counterterrorism, I don't want my puss plastered all over TV."

"I'll make all of your thoughts clear to the White House. I get the impression that the First Lady isn't crazy about the idea either.

"Now, can anybody enlighten me about this imam's idea that something big is on the way?"

"We've told you all about Imam Mike, our friend from Brooklyn," said Buster. "He's the best inside mole we've ever had. Director Carlini insisted that we put him on our payroll with a secret bank account, but Mike flatly refused. The guy isn't looking for money, he's looking to right some wrongs. If it wasn't for Mike, we wouldn't have known about either the spray bottles or the Baltimore factory. He also gave us inside information about people involved in Ellen Bellamy's kidnapping last year. So when Imam Mike says the shit is about to hit the fan, I duck. Problem is, we have no idea what they're up to. Mike will feed us information as soon as he gets it."

"So right now we have no idea when the event or events will happen, only that it will be a big one," said Watson.

"Let me put the word 'big' in perspective," I said. "We've seen the attacks of 10/15, the sinking of two cruise ships, two college football stadiums destroyed, and the Super Bowl disaster. Then there was the loss of the nuclear submarine, which we believe was terror related, and the bombing of that elementary school in New York, not to mention the attacks with The Scent of Revenge. If Imam Mike thinks something big is coming, I guarantee it won't be small."

"Well, guys, always a pleasure chatting with you folks about the mayhem in the world. I have to get back to Washington. It was great seeing all of you."

"Sarah," said Barbara Auletta, "I usually let my people talk for themselves, but I know I speak for everyone in this room when I say it's great to have you back." We stood and applauded.

Watson brushed away a tear as she opened the door.

# CHAPTER FIFTY-EIGHT

I walked into our apartment at 6:30. Ellen was on the phone having an animated conversation with somebody.

"It's for you, honey," said Ellen.

"Who is it?"

"Some guy from Washington named Reynolds."

She handed me the phone, laughing.

"Good evening, Mr. President," I said, as I pinched Ellen on the ass.

"Rick, I have an important matter to discuss with you. Please be in my office tomorrow at noon. A car will pick you up at 9:30 tomorrow morning. By the way, I just had a great conversation with your charming wife. The Bellamy Foundation will be an inspiration to the country. See you tomorrow, Rick."

I hung up the phone and turned back to Ellen.

"So what did the president want? I can't believe I picked up the phone and he was on the other end. He didn't even have a secretary place his call."

"That's signature Reynolds, hon. He loves the direct touch. He wants to see me at the White House tomorrow at noon. He says it's important."

⊰⊱

Ever since Ellen and the First Lady were stricken with *The Syndrome* within days of each other, President Reynolds seems to have taken a liking to me. I can't say that I'm not flattered, but he seems to have a trust in me that makes me feel honored. I'm a big fan of his. He's smart and he's tough, two important characteristics the country needs right now. I would have actively worked on his campaign, but that's strictly forbidden for FBI agents.

An aide met me at the entrance to the White House and escorted me to the Oval Office. I keep reminding myself that I'm an FBI agent, not a prima donna. But it's not easy to be cool and calm when entering such a historic building. Okay, I had to admit it to myself. I felt important.

"Great to see you again, Rick. Please have a seat. Coffee?"

"No thank you, Mr. President."

"I'll come right to the point, Rick. I want you to become a member of my cabinet, specifically as Secretary of Homeland Security. Our current secretary is stepping down. It can be a shit job, Rick, as I'm sure you've noticed in the years since the post was created in 2003. Whatever goes wrong, and things go wrong every day, some people will blame it on you. Sunday morning talking heads will rip your ass apart just for sport. But I'm not worried about it because you're one tough guy. I've been following your career for a while, and I need a brass pair of balls like yours on my cabinet. You're the best FBI agent we have on counterterrorism, Rick, and Homeland Security and counterterrorism are becoming almost synonymous."

Holy shit, he's asking me to be a cabinet secretary. Rick Bellamy, grunt FBI agent, is about to become Washington brass.

"Do you accept, Rick?"

"Yes, sir! I don't see how I could not. I think my skin is thick enough to put up with the critics," I said, hoping that I really believed what I was saying.

"A big part of the job, Rick, is to be square with the American people, and to calm things down when the shit hits the fan."

I was blown away. Me, Secretary of Homeland Security.

"You won't regret your decision, Mr. President." Kind of a lame comment, but I thought it seemed like an appropriate thing to say.

"Jack Conklin, my Chief of Staff, will fill you in on the details that you need to know. Welcome to the Reynolds Administration, Rick. I'm glad to have you on my team."

⊸┼ ┼⊷

It was June 24. What an amazing few weeks it had been. In early April, almost three months before, I lost my Ellen to a bizarre mental disease. Then she came back, smarter than ever. Now I'm Secretary of Homeland Security.

I called Ellen to tell her what time my flight would arrive in New York. She asked me to tell her what the meeting was all about, but I said that I wanted to tell her in person.

I arrived at our apartment at 6:15. Ellen greeted me at the door with a hug and a kiss.

"I'm bursting. What was the White House visit all about?"

"You're looking at the new Secretary of Homeland Security, hon. Your old man is now a cabinet officer."

"Holy shit, that is so outrageously wonderful. I'm so proud of you! You'll be on TV all the time. Tell me all about it."

"Well, a cabinet post doesn't pay quite as much as a partnership at Whitney, Cox, and Bellamy, but yes, my puss will be on TV a lot. I take my oath next Friday at the Oval Office."

"The Oval friggin Office? Pardon me while I faint."

"You'll be with me of course."

"Oh my God! I'll be with my Rick in the Oval Office. I hope Amanda Reynolds will be there. We've become close email buddies."

"The only problem is that my office will be in Washington, but I'll be spending a lot of time in New York, because that's where the FBI counterterrorism happens."

"And I'll come visit you in Washington. Our firm gets a lot of assignments in D.C. I'll talk to Phil Whitney about assigning some to me. I'm so friggin proud of you, Rick. Do Buster and Bennie know?"

"No, and please don't tell them. The White House likes to make dramatic announcements. Barbara Auletta has been briefed already."

# CHAPTER FIFTY-NINE

On Friday, July 1, I was sworn in as Secretary of Homeland Security. My parents and Ellen's parents were there. Also on hand were Bennie and Buster, and all the big TV networks and major newspapers. I had to admit, it felt cool.

After we all had lunch in the White House dining room, I met with Bennie and Buster in my new office nearby.

"We're going to miss having you around, Mr. Secretary," said Buster.

"The name's Rick, and you two are going to see more of me than you ever did. The most important part of my new job is counterterrorism, and that's where you two come in. Bennie, welcome to the bullshit capital of the world. I'm going to need your advice more than ever. And, Buster, I know you love to take action and see results. That's exactly what I'm planning. President Reynolds wants Homeland Security to work more closely with the FBI and CIA, so you'll be seeing a lot of me."

"Rick," said Buster, "are you thinking of doing things beyond what we're doing already?"

"Yes, we're going on offense. I don't like the plan that I'm about to describe to you guys," I said. "As a matter of fact, I hate it. But we're at war, and I've decided to play rough. Simply put, we have to get inside. Imam Mike is our best source for now, but we're going to need hundreds of Imam Mikes. Buster, I want to hear your thoughts."

"Imam Mikes are in short supply. We do have a few insiders, who I really can't discuss, but—"

"Can't discuss?" I said.

"Oh shit, sorry, Rick. I forgot that you're now a cabinet secretary. You have a need to know—*everything.*"

"Maybe I should get out of here, guys," said Bennie.

"No," I said. "Bennie, psychological profiles will be a major part of our offensive. I need you, and I need you to know what's going on. So getting back to Buster, tell us about our inside efforts."

"The news isn't good. We have exactly 77 people who I count on as good moles, only 77 people, including Imam Mike, who's the best. Remember that guy Smitty who helped us raid the al-Qaeda safe house where Ellen was a hostage? We need more people like him, great people, but in short supply."

"Talk to me about recruiting. What more can we do?"

"I think I'll to defer to our psychiatrist friend here on that one, Rick. Remember, we're talking about a strong pull of a religion and ideology, and that's not easy to crack. Imam Mike had his own epiphany. He saw the light all by himself. He got fed up with senseless killing and came over to the side of enlightenment. We didn't recruit him. He recruited himself. What do you think, Bennie?"

"Well, *The New York Times* carried an article recently about a group of eight young men from a small town in Norway called Fredrikstad. Out of a population of around 75,000 people, eight kids went to Syria to fight alongside ISIS. Eight kids from one small fucking town. Let's take a look at ground zero of the jihadist mind, the place where twisted radical ideas take root. There was a time

207

when we could spy on radical websites and track suspects with the CIA's brilliant algorithm. But, as we all know, the jihadis are on to us, and they've gone underground. We've been calling their new procedures The Shadows of Terror. They avoid radical websites. Shit, as we've learned from Mike, they even avoid going to mosques. They've learned to hide in the shadows."

"So what do you think is the *new* ground zero of radicalism?" I said.

"It isn't new," said Bennie, "but it's the one place where they don't lurk in shadows, and that's prisons. We've all heard countless times about a jihadi who became radicalized in prison. Bill O'Reilly recently talked on his show about a man named Faud al-Bayly who called for the death of that Islam reformer woman Ayaan Hirsi Ali. That son of a bitch was actually hired by the State Department to preach Islam in prisons. And you've heard me say this before: a mind can become radicalized over the craziest of reasons. As we saw with the 10/15 bombers, it could be a slight, an insult, or something in a person's life that creates a mind that's ripe for revenge. A lot of killers went to prison without any religious belief at all, and then came out the other end totally swayed by a religious ideology from the dark ages. It's a simple way for a criminal to give meaning to a wasted, disaffected life. Does that mean they're psychopaths? Yeah, frankly, a lot of them are."

"So give me a concrete suggestion, Ben."

"We need to put our people in prisons. We need eyes and ears. All they have to do is look, listen, and report. Once they tell us about a newborn radical about to get out, we put the guy into Buster's database and watch him—or her. There are 1,800 state and federal prisons in the country and 3,200 local and county jails. If we just concentrate on the state and federal prisons, where people serve longer sentences, we'll need 1,800 inside spies. Buster says we only have 77 moles that we can count on. We have a lot of recruiting to do."

"But how the hell do we convince people to go to a prison voluntarily as a spy?" I said.

"We need to pay them well and make their assignments of a short duration," Bennie said. "To count on a regular turnover, we need a lot more than 1,800 people. I hope you've got friends on the Ways and Means Committee, Rick. We're gonna need one hell of a budget."

"This can work," said Buster. "The people we've been recruiting up till now all speak Arabic, a primary qualification. Since Bennie is talking about putting the eye on home-grown jihadis, we don't need Arabic speakers. And we don't need combat-tested recruits. Their only job is to watch, listen, and report. We can do this."

"I have one final question for this meeting," I said. "So we follow Bennie's plan and identify radicalized prisoners who are about to get out. Then what do we do, put surveillance on each one of them? If we want to use tracking devices, we'll need a FISA court order."

"Well, Mr. Secretary," said Buster, "we now have a powerful and persuasive man in charge. That would be you."

"Okay, guys, time to lock and load."

# CHAPTER SIXTY

"Peace be with you, Brother Pashez. Welcome to The Committee," said Ali Muqtada, who was sitting at the head of a table of 12 other men.

"And peace be with you, Brother Ali. But should I not be called by my infidel name, Howard Orlando?"

"Here in Yemen, we do not worry about such things, but when you are in America, you're right to be cautious.

"So please bring The Committee up to date on our plans for next year," said Muqtada.

"Our research shows that our plan will be the most ambitious we have ever undertaken," said Pashez. "It will make all of the events since October 15 seem like minor incidents. Even the Super Bowl or our attacks with The Scent of Revenge will pale in comparison."

"Please be specific, Brother."

"I shall be quite specific. We have studied the American electric grid, and it is surprisingly vulnerable, but that does not give us confidence. Yes, it is vulnerable, and the list of targets can be quite small. Taking them out will do an enormous amount of damage.

The country has three large regional power grids, but they have limited connectivity between them. This means that if one goes down, it cannot easily take power from one of the other grids. Of the 55,000 electric-transmission substations, only nine are critical. Attacking these nine substations and taking them off the grid can plunge America into darkness that will last for months, as long as 18 months, according to our calculations. Also, there are only a handful of companies in America that manufacture the huge transformers that are necessary. If we attack the substations and also attack the transformer manufacturers, the result could be chaos. Unless they can replace the transformers, we may be thinking in terms of years of darkness."

"But, Brother Pashez," said Muqtada, "I am getting the impression that you are not enthusiastic about attacking the American electric grid. Am I wrong, or do you doubt the plan?"

"No, Ali, you are not wrong. I have serious doubts. All of the planning we've done to date assumes that the infidels are stupid. They are not. The ill-conceived attack on the electric substation in California in 2013 resulted in more newspaper and magazine articles than we could have imagined. The attack was daring. The brothers who took part in the raid opened fire on 17 electric transformers, taking them out. The shooting went on for almost 20 minutes. It took almost a month for the Americans to get the station back on line. Before the police arrived, the brothers escaped. The articles discussed the problem with the grid and its vulnerabilities. To put it simply, the Americans are aware that they have a problem; and when they are aware of a problem, they are vigilant. The California incident put them on notice, and we have to assume that they have come up with secret plans to avoid such a disaster in the future."

"So, if I'm hearing you correctly, you have concluded that the electric grid attack has a high risk of failure," said Muqtada.

"Yes, that is exactly what I am saying," said Pashez. "So much time, money, and people would be involved that the risk of failure has convinced me that we should abandon the plan. If the plan were intercepted somehow, all of our other plans would be put off far into the future."

"And what have you come up with to replace this glorious plan, Brother Pashez? Do you expect us to remain quiet for a while?"

"No, Brother Muqtada. Our new plan will be the most ambitious one we've ever launched, more ambitious than 9/11 and even 10/15. Our new plan will be unlike anything else we've ever discussed. It will be relentless, non-stop, and designed to bring the infidels to their knees, begging for mercy, which, of course, we will not give them."

"Please be specific, Brother Pashez."

"It has already begun, my brother. Two years ago, we began a quiet recruiting campaign, assisted by our new policy of waging jihad in the shadows. Some of the heathen FBI and CIA people have called it The Shadows of Terror. It's nothing new that we have recruited martyrs from prisons, but the difference is the scale. In the past year alone, we have brought 3,000 young men, and a few women, into the embrace of Allah. Our plan is huge, vast, but it is also quite simple. Call it a death by a thousand cuts. Every day in America, there will be at least five, and sometimes as many as 20 or more, incidents of jihad, carried out by our new and growing army of recruits."

"But," said Muqtada, "with so many newcomers, is not the chance of discovery great? How can so many be counted on to remain silent, or remain in the shadows?"

"We have anticipated that problem and I believe we have it solved. The cells in which these recruits will operate will be extremely small, no more than six people, including a cell leader. If a cell is infiltrated, it will not matter, because the leader of cell A will have no knowledge of the plans of Cell B. So even if a cell member or leader is captured and tortured, they will have no information to share."

"And what about the senior leadership, Brother Pashez? How many top level leaders will be involved, and how can we prevent their capture?"

"The answer is 20, Brother Muqtada. There will be 20 top leaders. I have their names for you here on this list. I'm sure you will recognize most of them, and you'll agree that they are trustworthy."

"They may be trustworthy, but how can we make certain that none of them will be compromised? It's happened before."

"Now I will tell you about the true beauty of the plan. The actions of these martyrs will be small, with small amounts of explosives, guns, knives, or poisons. The top leaders, the 20, will have no knowledge of the plans of the individual cells. That's right, the operations will be totally diffuse, with no central brother giving the commands. He will not give the commands, because he will not know of the plans to command."

"And what of us, Brother Pashez? What about The Committee? What about you?"

"I will learn, as you will learn, just what the plans will be at the moment they happen. There will be a bomb set off on a crowded sidewalk in New York City, a train platform explosion in Chicago, a blast in a shopping center in Los Angeles. There will be a knifing in one city in the morning, and a random shooting in another city at noon. The only rule for the leaders is this: pick no targets that are covered by any kind of security. That means that bombs on trains are out, as, of course, bombs on planes. But there can never be security among simple crowds of people, and that will be our primary targets, or I should say, that will be our suggestion to the leaders and the cell leaders. Just general guidelines."

"I can begin to see the result. Enlighten me with your thoughts, brother."

"The simple word, Brother Muqtada, is terror. I am less concerned about how many infidels we kill than about how many of them we frighten. People will be afraid to turn on their TVs or radios, for fear of hearing about that morning's attacks, fully knowing that they will be followed up by more in the afternoon and evening. We saw this after our glorious attacks of 10/15, but the sheer number will make 10/15 look like a slow news day. People will be afraid to shop, to go to their offices or businesses. Soon, they will fear leaving their homes. The American economy will be crippled. So what are your thoughts, Brother Muqtada?"

"America will become a vast wasteland."

# CHAPTER SIXTY-ONE

I visited the New York office of the FBI at 26 Federal Plaza to meet with Barbara Auletta. She asked why I didn't just call her to Washington, but I said that I also wanted to visit with Bennie and Buster. That was a white lie. I wanted to go to New York to be with Ellen.

I got to our apartment at 6:30. Ellen was already there, which was great. Coming home to that empty apartment while Ellen resided at New Horizons Nursing Home was the worst experience of my life.

She greeted me at the door with our wonderful ritual. After we kissed, I had to get something off my chest.

"There's one thing about my new job that sucks, Ellen—being away from you. When you got your life back after you were cured of *The Syndrome*, I got my life back too. That's because you *are* my life. So much of my time is tied up in Washington that I spend entirely too much of my life away from the most important person in my world."

She held my face in both of her hands and kissed me.

"After what you just said, I think I have the perfect gift for you. Rick, you're looking at the new managing partner of the Washington D.C. office of Whitney, Cox, and Bellamy. Phil Whitney broke it to me this afternoon. With some of my big MacPherson bonus money, we can pay off the mortgage on this condo and keep it. It'll be kind of neat to have an apartment in New York and one in D.C. You'll have to be in New York from time to time and so will I."

"So, what shall we do to celebrate?"

"Well, Mr. Secretary, I was thinking that we should get naked, shower, and make love till the wee hours."

"Your executive decision-making is inspiring," I said, as I unbuttoned her blouse.

# CHAPTER SIXTY-TWO

The past few weeks of our lives were a blur. I lost Ellen and then she came back. She didn't just come back, my life came back. To cap things off, I was appointed Secretary of Homeland Security. One thing we never have to worry about is boredom. The Bellamy Foundation is fast becoming one of the best-funded charities in the country. With Ellen as the key spokesperson, the money gushes in from all sides. Our Board of Trustees includes Dr. Frank Buchannan, the man who discovered the cure for *The Syndrome*, and Dr. Harry Noonan, the nation's leading expert on Alzheimer's. Angus MacPherson is also on the board. Because his daughter Jane was one of the victims of *The Syndrome*, Angus took a special interest in The Bellamy Foundation. With a vast army of subcontractors who rely on MacPherson International for business, Angus is responsible for an avalanche of donations. Ellen, who serves as Chairman of the Board, more than earns her $1.00 a year salary.

Even with her crazy schedule, Ellen quizzes me every day about my daily routine of exercise, meditation, and yes, I still look at a

Seinfeld joke before picking up the phone. And number one on our list, making love, gives the whole project a wonderful meaning.

Having apartments in New York and Washington was one of our best decisions. Besides convenience, it meant that Ellen and I would seldom be apart for long. After her weeks in mental wilderness with *The Syndrome*, and my weeks of despair, the thought of being away from Ellen for extended periods sickened me.

On a Saturday in late July, Ellen and I enjoyed some quiet time together at our new apartment in Washington. With Ellen's busy architectural schedule, not to mention her work with our foundation and my responsibilities at Homeland Security, it's rare when we can just sit alone with each other and talk. We put our cell phones on mute. I left my emergency phone on, which my position requires.

We sat on our new sofa. A large window in the room gave us a stunning view of the Capitol Building. I turned the lights low, and we held hands.

"I'm so proud of you, Rick. I saw you on TV yesterday being interviewed on Fox. I couldn't help thinking that our country is safe with this man."

"That's sweet of you to say, hon, but even though I'm near the top of the pecking order, our security depends on a lot of people, a lot more than me."

"Hey, let's look at the bright side, Rick. There hasn't been a terrorist incident in the States for over six weeks."

"I don't know if that's a bright side or a dark side. We know something's coming. According to our imam friend from Brooklyn, the jihadis are planning something big."

"Rick, all you can do is plan and pray for the best. We can't obsess about it."

"You're the only thing I want to obsess about."

"Well, I have some great news to take our obsessive minds off the world's mayhem. I just landed a major project from the Four Seasons hotel chain. They're planning a huge new hotel in D.C. and they approached your humble wife personally. Angus MacPherson referred them to me. A rough calculation tells me that my fee alone should be over $3 million. And that doesn't count my regular partnership profits."

I grew up in a middle-class family in Queens, New York. Our idea of a big vacation was a trip to the Poconos. My dad worked for Con Edison, the utility, as an accountant, and mom was a school teacher. We never wanted for anything, but luxuries came only occasionally. I had a hard time processing the number that Ellen just tossed out—$3 million for one project.

"You know, hon," I said, "I have a crazy feeling that our lives have calmed down nicely since the past few weeks. As you said, terror attacks are down, and I think we can be happy that things are becoming normal, whatever the hell normal is. My job is to expect the worst, but, for now, I think I'll just hold hands with my favorite person."

My secure phone rang. "Bellamy here."

"Mr. Secretary, I suggest you turn on the TV if it's not on already."

"This is Harris Faulkner reporting for Fox News, ladies and gentlemen, interrupting our regular program. We're getting a flood of reports, very upsetting reports, about a rash of apparent terror attacks in just the past 10 minutes. Bombs have been set off in busy shopping center parking lots in New York, San Francisco, Denver, and Kansas City. There have been at least six random stabbings, and five shootings, all in crowded areas. At least three suicide bombers have detonated themselves on crowded buses in Miami, Boston, and Philadelphia. That makes 18 acts of terror in the past 10 minutes."

I put the TV on mute. Ellen stared into my eyes.

"I know, I know. You have to go to the office. I want to come with you. I can be helpful, even if it just means being with you to help keep you calm."

I called for my car.

"Yes, come with me. I want you to be surrounded by tight security. Last year you were kidnapped and this year you were taken down with *The Syndrome*. The closer you are to me, the better I'll feel. I'm going to get you appointed as a consultant to Homeland Security. God knows we can use your brains. It will be an unpaid position, to avoid me having to explain it to the world every Sunday morning, but it will keep you in the loop, and most importantly, you'll be surrounded by armed security."

We stood in the lobby with my two body guards, waiting for my car. Ellen grabbed my hand.

"Rick, we don't know a lot yet, but do you think these reports mean something new? I've never heard of so many attacks in such a short period of time."

"Yes, I think it does mean something, hon. We've been worried about this for a long time, and I think we're seeing it happen. They're adopting a strategy of 'death by a thousand cuts.' They're going to hit us in small, relentless attacks, the kind of attacks that are almost impossible to predict. I think they're giving up on big risky spectaculars, like the 9/11, 10/15, or The Scent of Revenge. They're going to pull off a lot of small attacks, a lot. Add them up and you have a terror spectacular every week. I've told my staff that I want to go on offense, but how the hell do I go on offense when I can't see the enemy until he hits. Unless I've got some data screaming at me from our intelligence, I don't know what I've got."

Ellen put her face next to my ear and spoke softly.

"Yes you do, hon. You've got me."

# CAST OF CHARACTERS –
## *THE SCENT OF REVENGE*

Adams, Maria –Deputy Secretary of State

Atkins, Charles – CIA agent. See also, Buster

Auletta, Barbara – FBI agent and head of the New York Bureau

Bellamy, Ellen – Architect. Rick Bellamy's wife

Bellamy, Rick – FBI agent. Head of counterterrorism unit

Buchannan, Frank – Epidemiologist – Medical detective

Burns, Olga – Home aide and caregiver

Busharif, Muhammed (Mike) – Imam and FBI/CIA mole

Buster – CIA agent, aka Charles Atkins

Carlini, William – Director of the CIA

Conklin, Jack – White House Chief of Staff

Copeland, Melanie – Reporter, NBC News

Flynn, Joe – FBI database expert

Frankel, Don – FBI driver, Baltimore

Giovanni, Marla – Vice President, Microsoft

Johnston, Angela – President, University of Michigan

Langdon, Nancy – Nurse, New Horizons Nursing Home

Langston, Jerome – Police officer

Logan, Bonnie – Homicide detective and wife of Jack Logan

Logan, Jack – FBI agent, Philadelphia office

MacPherson, Angus – Real estate developer
McCue, Roger. Lt. Cdr. – Submarine weapons officer, aka Ali Shabana
McLaughlin, Bob – Photographer and drone pilot
McMartin, Trevor – Australian bank examiner
Mousell, Yousef – Window washer
Muqtada, Ali – Terrorist leader
Noonan, Harry – Physician, expert in Alzheimer's disease
Orlando, Howard – Terrorist leader
Paddington, Joan – CEO of Megasoft
Pashez, Gamal – Terrorist leader
Patterson, Ashley – Rear Admiral, United States Navy
Pushkin, Dmitri – Chemistry Professor
Reynolds, Amanda – First Lady of the United States
Reynolds, William – President of the United States
Richardson, Derek – Linebacker, New York Giants
Rugirello, Bill – Cruise ship officer
Simmons, Randolph – Captain, United States Navy, aide to Admiral Patterson
Thompson, Jimmy – Cargo ship captain, aka Islam Yamani
Thorssen, Magnus – Cruise ship captain
Townsend, Regina – President, New York Stock Exchange
Watson, Sarah – Director of the FBI
Weinberg, Bennie – Psychiatrist and NYPD Detective
Yates, Darryl – Chicago Police Commissioner

# ABOUT THE AUTHOR

Russ Moran is the author of *The Gray Ship* (Coddington Press, 2013), Book One of *The Time Magnet* series. It's a story of time travel, romance, and a nuclear warship that finds itself in the Civil War. *The Thanksgiving Gang* is the sequel, *A Time of Fear* is Book Three, and *The Skies of Time* is Book Four in the series.

This book, *The Scent of Revenge*, is the second book in the Patterns Series, the sequel to *The Shadows of Terror*.

Russ Moran has also published five nonfiction books: *Justice in America: How it Works—How it Fails* (Coddington Press, 2011); *The APT Principle: The Business Plan That You Carry in Your Head* (Coddington Press, 2012); *Boating Basics: The Boattalk Book of Boating Tips* (Coddington Press, 2013); *If You're Injured: A Consumer Guide to Personal Injury Law* (Coddington Press, 2013); *How to Create More Time* (Coddington Press, 2014). He's a lawyer and a veteran of the United States Navy. He lives on Long Island, New York, with his wife, Lynda.

If you enjoyed *The Scent of Revenge*, please consider leaving a review on amazon.com.

Russ Moran's next book, *Sideswiped,* will appear in the summer of 2015. It's a legal thriller and a romance.

To make sure you don't miss out on Russ Moran's forthcoming books, visit his website, http://www.morancom.com, and click on the "subscribe and get updates button."

# THE BOOKS OF
# RUSSELL F. MORAN

***The Gray Ship*** – Book One of *The Time Magnet Series*
http://amzn.to/16GPumH

"This provocative, intensely powerful novel is a must-read for sci-fi fans and Civil War aficionados, though mainstream fiction readers will find it heart-rending and inspiring as well. A rare read that's not only wildly entertaining, but also profoundly moving." ~Kirkus Reviews

***The Thanksgiving Gang*** – Book Two of *The Time Magnet Series* http://amzn.to/1NzBs7N

"I had never read a book before written in an efficient, minimalistic prose... Instead of writing what most readers want to read, he gives voice to life-like characters, with their flaws and prejudices. They are not infallible superheroes. It's always nice to find a new voice in fiction and to enjoy creativity at its best." ~C. Ludewig

***A Time of Fear*** – Book Three of *The Time Magnet Series*
http://amzn.to/1zdjaG9

"His story is fascinating, and adds even more depth to this already cavernously deep novel. Amazingly unique, chilling and well written, Moran weaves a future that is both desperate and hopeful. Blending modern fears with science fiction results in a tale that will keep you reading long into the night. Five stars!" ~Heather

**The Skies of Time** – Book Four of *The Time Magnet Series*
http://amzn.to/1CCC3jg

In *The Skies of Time,* you will recognize the two main characters, Ashley Patterson, now an admiral, and her husband, Jack Thurber. They met and fell in love in *The Gray Ship*, and now they're in for the adventure of their lives in *The Skies of Time*. Ashley and Jack have been such prominent characters in all four books of The Time Magnet Series that I feel like they're old friends. You will also recognize some of the other characters. But if I told you who they are, it would ruin the fun.

*The Skies of Time* is a novel of time travel. Naturally, the book is fiction, but I've tried to make it as realistic as possible. Ashley and Jack are faced with the big question that troubles all time travelers—dare they change history? As the author, I'm the last one to be a spoiler, so I'll leave the answer to the characters in the book.

"I'm big fan of this series and this one may be the best. I hope there is another book to this series since it keeps getting better. There is a few questions I have about certain events that makes the next one even more suspenseful. These are great books to binge read one after the other." ~ Time Travel Fan

**The Shadows of Terror** – Book One of the *Patterns Series*
http://amzn.to/1IDQzJS

A novel that explodes off the front page of your newspaper.

Terrorism now has a new face, a face that's obscured in the shadows. The radical forces of destruction have learned to make themselves invisible to the West, and preventing a terrorist attack has become almost impossible.

A new war has begun, World War III.

Rick Bellamy, an FBI agent who specializes in counterterrorism, is engaged in his own war, a war with no end.

Bellamy's wife, Ellen, a prominent architect, discovers that she's in the middle of the greatest terror plot to date.

To defeat the enemy, Bellamy first has to uncover the clues, to shine a light on the shadows. He has to find patterns – before it's too late.

"Move over James Patterson and Mary Higgins Clark. There's a new guy in town. Russ Moran's new book – *The Shadows of Terror.*" ~ Frank from Lynbrook

**The Scent of Revenge,** the book you've just read, is Book Two in the *Patterns Series*. Please consider leaving a brief review of *The Scent of Revenge* on Amazon.

www.ingramcontent.com/pod-product-compliance
Lightning Source LLC
Chambersburg PA
CBHW070104260626
47160CB00004B/1315